Shades

MADE IN MICHIGAN WRITERS SERIES

GENERAL EDITORS

Michael Delp, Interlochen Center for the Arts

M. L. Liebler, Wayne State University

A complete listing of the books in this series can be found online at
wsupress.wayne.edu

Advance praise for *Shades*

"Esperanza Cintron really drew me close to her characters. I was enthralled by them, moved by their tragedies, and I enjoyed their lust for life. I caught myself asking why they get into these predicaments but then it is all there, it made sense. Before I knew it, I had reached the end of the book. What a read."

—Osvaldo "Ozzie" Rivera, musician and cultural activist

"We are invited into a world in which characters and their tales, over extended spans of time, connect and interweave with the intricate delicacy of a sunlit spider's web. I wish I had written them."

—Bill Harris, 2011 Kresge Foundation Eminent Artist
and author of *I Got to Keep Moving*
(Wayne State University Press, 2018)

"In this vibrant collection of interconnected stories, Cintrón captures the struggles, joys, funk, suffering, and transcendence of a hard-living and hard-loving community and its people. So many characters left the page and lingered in my consciousness; so many shades of wonderful."

—Cecilia Rodríguez Milanés, author of
Oye What I'm Gonna Tell You

"A richly textured tapestry of the lived experiences of ordinary working-class Detroiters, men and women, the young and the young-at-heart, that brings to light the daily struggles of the disenfranchised and marginalized who strive to eke out a living; put a roof over their heads; care for their loved ones; fend off racism, crime, and urban blight; and keep hope alive through spiritual salvation, education, and love in one of America's postindustrial cities."

—Jorge L. Chinea, professor of history
and director of the Center for
Latino/a and Latin American Studies

Shades

Detroit Love Stories

Esperanza Cintrón

WAYNE STATE UNIVERSITY PRESS
DETROIT

ISBN 978-0-8143-4688-4 (paperback)
ISBN 978-0-8143-4689-1 (e-book)

Library of Congress Control Number: 2019936419

Publication of this book was made possible by a generous gift from The Meijer Foundation. This work is supported in part by an award from the Michigan Council for Arts and Cultural Affairs.

Wayne State University Press
Leonard N. Simons Building
4809 Woodward Avenue
Detroit, Michigan 48201–1309

Visit us online at wsupress.wayne.edu

To Suzy
the Belle of Detroit
and to Vince
who loved me
when I needed to be loved

Contents

shade/shades

shade *n*/SHād/shades *pl* (EBO ndò shade, shelter; GK skotos darkness; SP sombra shadow, sueño dream; YRI iboji shade, shadow, tomb, grave) 1: Spanish painter Francisco Goya, known for his horrific *Saturn Devouring His Son*, said that in art there is no need for color. He saw only light and shade, and boasted that, if given one crayon, he could paint anyone's portrait. 2: duskiness, a dimness due to the disruption of light, a darkening. 3: a: shelter from sunlight and the resulting coolness, b: a place to sprawl or cower. 4: a fleeting, unreal appearance. 5: *pl* the shadows that gather as darkness comes, akin to Sheol, Hades, the under- or netherworld. 6: a spirit, ghost, a haint. 7: a screen or shield from light or heat, as in a lampshade or sunglasses. 8: a slight difference or variation, as in degree or quantity, nuance. 9 a: color produced by a pigment or mixture having some black in it, b: a color slightly different from another. 10: a tone, tint, a tinge, as in the American actress Carole Lombard's declaration that she lived by a man's code but could never forget that a woman's first job was to choose the right shade of lipstick. 11: a facial expression of displeasure or sadness.

shade *vb*; shad-ing; shad-ed, shad-y *adj* 1: to screen, cover, shelter. 2: British author/artist Wyndham Lewis maintained that the natural state of man is a wormlike movement from a spot of sunlight to a spot of shade, and back again. 3: to hide. 4: to darken. 5: to lessen or diminish. 6: John Constable, 19th-century landscape painter, claimed that he'd never seen an ugly thing in his life. Let the form of an object be what it may, he asserted, and light, shade, and perspective will always make it beautiful. 7: to cast into shade (by overshadowing or acting superior). 8: to judge or disrespect, dissing or throwing shade as in the popular meme "Don't Like Me? Have a seat with the rest of the bitches waiting for me to give a fuck." 9: to be fake or phony, as in acting shady. 10: to color so that the shades pass little by little from one to another, to transition gradually. 11: to change by imperceptible degrees into something else.

Based on inference and The Ever-Unfolding Book of Life

Eastside

The Beard

Margaret

Belle come downstairs and ask me if I want to go to the bar with her. I tell her I don't feel like it, that I rather stay home and watch *Twilight Zone*, but she start in on me.

"Margaret girl, you gon dry up like them turnips you forgot you had in the bottom of your refrigerator."

"I just don't feel like sitting up in no bar half the night, listening to loud music while some drunk dude breathe his stale beer breath in my face," I tell her.

"Come on," she push. "We'll have a couple of drinks, listen to some music, and maybe dance some. When the last time you danced?" she ask and then add, "You might even meet somebody good."

I know Belle just want me with her as a shade, a cover to hide her real purpose. She just take me or Diane, the girl that live upstairs, to keep the bartender from catching on. But I figure, maybe I *might* meet somebody. Besides, I spend too many nights with Rod Serling. Listening to Smokey or Little Stevie and maybe dancing sound kinda good; I ain't danced since before I had Belinda.

Anyway, about ten, she come downstairs. I'm in my room getting dressed, but I hear her as soon as she come through the door talking about, "Girl, we gon miss everything. You better come on." Then she in my room rushing me, talking about ain't gon be nowhere left to sit if we get there too late. I got her number; she just don't want to miss none a that money.

The straight green dress she got on is hugging her hips so tight I can see the line of her panties. She must not be wearing no stockings cause I cain't see no garter belt. But the V-neck look kind of nice and won't show too much if she don't lean forward. She look a lot better than when she first came up here from down south wearing them high heels and anklets. Belle was a sight with a baby on her hip, three stair steps tugging on her skirt and that trifling husband trailing up behind her.

Smoothing down the back of her skirt, she sit down on my bed, knees together and legs slanted to the side, real ladylike, like in one of them magazines. I just smile and shake my head cause I know she practicing her part. I keep on getting dressed.

"Girl," she start in again. "You know them mens like them some yellow women. You could probably have your pick." I ignore her, pull my dress over my head, and tug the skirt part into place. "And you look pretty good when you get dressed up. You could really make some money if you would just make half a effort."

I laugh it off and finish putting on my stockings, making sure the last garter clip is secure before smoothing my skirt back down. She still talking, but I'm only half listening. I'm mostly trying to hear whether my girls is getting ready for bed like I told them to. I can hear Barbara showing Belinda how to brush her teeth. "Not so much toothpaste. Momma said just a little dab a do." I laugh and Belle's eyebrows go up in a question. Barbara saying, "Up and down, up and down, like this."

We hail a cab up on Woodward and head over to the Apex on Oakland. It's just a neighborhood bar, but the jukebox is always up-to-date and full of quarters. The music is loud, the drinks cheap, and they keep the lights low so you cain't see the dirt or the worn edges and split seats of the red leather benches in the booths. Belle say it's a magnet for working mens.

When we get there it's pretty crowded. All the little round tables in the front is full, and folks laughing and talking loud. B. B. King on the jukebox singing "The Thrill Is Gone," and a few couples is grinding on the tiny dance floor. Some mens is in the back paying up at the pool table, counting out dollar bills, while the next set is racking up the balls. I want to find a booth and just sit back and watch the folks, but Belle grab my elbow and drag me toward a couple of stools at the bar.

She take her time sliding onto the stool slow, deliberate-like, her back against the bar and her body aimed at the crowd. Then she pull out her Pell Mells, plop the pack onto the dark wood of the bar, and tell me to order us a couple a Buds. I walk down the bar a ways so I can catch the bartender's eye. The bottles are cold and wet; I set them on the coasters and put the glasses down next to them. Then I take my seat next to Belle, but I'm facing the bar.

Junior Walker's saxophone sound like he right here in the room. He start singing, "Shotgun, shoot 'em 'fore he run now," and some couples head to the tiny dance floor and start doing the jerk. Me and Belle sit awhile sipping our beer while Belle point out men who look like they might have some money. When one look her way, she smile, suck on her Pell Mell, and blow the smoke out real slow. Then she cross her legs trying to hold his attention. When he move on without stopping, she turn halfway back around to the bar and take a long swig of beer. I ask her why she drink her beer out the bottle, and she say it taste better that way. "Ladies supposed to drink out of a glass," I say. But she just twist her lips at me, shake her head, and make a sucking sound with her teeth.

The bass is bumping and the music sound good. Belle cracking on the dudes, talking about how this one need to buy a jar of Vaseline to grease his ashy arms or how that one need to either comb them naps or cut 'em off. She say, "Some mens just don't think they even have to try." She shake her head and tap her cigarette over the orange plastic ashtray.

I'm starting to feel the effects of the beer, a low even buzz that made Marvin Gaye sound like a angel when this big ole dude come up to me and start talking trash. He not exactly old, but he ain't too young, and he a big one. He ask me if I'm having a good time. I just nod, but he keep on talking like a gnat buzzing in my ear. I want to swat him. Belle giggle and whisper something about yellow being like honey to a bee. I shove her a little, warning her to behave. Not wanting to be rude, I smile back at the big fella and nod like I'm listening to what he saying. He ask me do I want another drink, and I say that me and my friend was just about to order another one. Raising his long arm to catch the bartender's eye, he hold up two fingers and wiggle them over our heads. Then he tell me his name Richard. I tell him mine and introduce him to Belle. He say he a truck driver, own his own rig. He say, "I'm celebrating making the last payment on my rig. Took me ten years, but I did it." I look at him, trying to read him. I ain't so good at reading men, but he look real. I nod, letting him know I'm listening. Then he tell me he live with his momma and daddy. "For the time being," he say. Just since him and his wife separated. I just nod again and let him talk. He looking less and less good, but listening is the least I can do since he buying us drinks.

He talk a lot, but I'm beginning to get interested. I like his warm, homey, open way, and he make me laugh. I like the way he feel standing over me, like a big, tame, cuddly bear.

I'd just about forgot about Belle when she ask did I have a quarter for the jukebox. Richard dig down in his pocket and come up with a handful a change. He hold a palm full of nickels, dimes, and quarters out to her. She take three or four quarters, say thanks, and sashay over to the jukebox.

Richard leaning over me; his big body all around me. The soft wool of his Italian knit sweater is brushing against my cheek. I don't mind because his broad chest is radiating a cozy heat that make me feel safe, and his voice is a soft hum in my ear. I feel a little guilty about liking it so much and for ignoring Belle. So, I peek around Richard to check on her. She over there hugging that jukebox, leaning so far over the glass that anybody who interested can peek up that short dress. And she grinding her hips to the music like the jukebox is her lover.

"Let's get that seat over there," Richard say, pointing to a booth near the back where the man is helping the lady with her sweater as they getting ready to leave. I nod, grab my beer, and let him take my hand and lead me through the crowd.

Belle

I shove the quarters into the slot, wait for the box to realize that I gave it some money, and then I lean in to pick my songs. I told that silly yellow bitch that what she got is like honey. She over there nodding and giggling at that big dude, and he all wrapped around her like he want to climb up inside her. She playing games. Cain't she see he got a pocket full of money, and just dying to give it away. I swear some folks so stupid it make me mad. But hey, ain't no skin off my nose. I just brought her here to keep the bartender off my ass. Besides, I knew that innocent act of hers would draw these mens out. Now I'm gon pick something slow and sexy and reel 'em in.

My girl, Etta James, always do the trick. I punch the buttons and step back to watch the record as it tip up and then slide onto the spindle. Besides, the blacker the berry, the sweeter the juice, and I know this blackberry look good tonight. I lean in to pick another record as Etta's words float out slow and sultry, "At last, my love has come along." I lean into the box; its glass hood is hard and steady against my stomach, and the music is a throb, trembling through my body. "My lonely days are over, and life is like a song." Etta wailing.

"Hey, momma, it got to be a sin for one woman to look as good as you do." The words come from behind me. They pull me away from Etta, but I take my time lifting myself off the jukebox before I say, "Why thank you, baby," and let him talk a little more shit. He go on about how I smell sweet as the flowers in his grandmother's garden and how I look good enough to eat. Then he ask how come a woman as fine as me standing here all by myself.

His suit kinda cheap, but his shoes got a shine on 'em. He steady nudging me up against the wall, pretending like we dancing, all the time smiling, showing his two gold teeth that he got right in the front of his mouth. I smile too, lowering my eyes shy-like, playing the game. All the while, I'm wanting to laugh at this country fool. He talking about I look like the kinda girl make a niggah fall in love. He close enough to kiss me now, but I turn my head, and he tell me again about how sweet I smell.

We dance to another slow one, and this niggah so hard, I hope he don't come while we dancing. I won't let him slow drag like he want to. Instead, I make him move his feet.

He talking plenty shit now while he try to lead me into the back near the pay phone where it's darkest. Telling me all he want to do to me.

I say, "People in hell want ice water."

He say, "Baby, don't be so cold," and start kissing me on my neck.

My dress is kinda low in the front so he headed that way. His lips tickling me, and I want to laugh cause he trying so hard, but I just bear it and even moan a little. He amp it up, telling me how soft I am, and how good he know I must be.

I nod and say, "Yeah, baby, I'm good."

Then he ask do I have a man, and I tell him that it don't matter, but I got kids, and I don't fuck for free.

He stop kissing for a minute and look at me with a little sneaky grin. Then he kiss the crease between my titties and ask how much. I tell him twenty the regular way, and he say, "Let's go."

We go over across the street. I got this arrangement with the lady who rent rooms over the hardware store. It's just a bed in a empty room, but she change the sheets before they get too bad, and it's cheap. Besides, she don't make you sign your name or nothing, and she mind her own business. Anyway, we get there and this niggah try to get his and a couple a other folk's money's worth. I mean, first he rush in and claim I got him so hot he cain't wait. Then he on me for what seem like half the night. Finally, he come, and then he just flop down on me like he got cement in his ass. I push him off me, and he roll over, acting like he sleep. I sit up and light up a Pell Mell.

After a while, I ask the trick for my money, and he look up at me with this shit-eating grin and tell me he ain't got no twenty dollars. He tell me he know I liked it, and then he say I probably should be paying him. I look at this mothafuckah, and I get cold. I mean, for real. My toes and fingers start icing up. I say, "What did you say, mothafuckah?" Cause I know he joking. But he still laying there grinning up at me.

"You gon do me like that?" I look at him straight-faced so he know I'm serious. "Steal from me like that and expect me to just take it?"

He laugh and shake his head like I'm the funniest thing he ever seen.

Well, I don't even have to think about it. There is only one thing I can do.

So, I get up, put on my clothes, not too fast, not too slow. Give him time to make things right. He don't, so I reach for my purse. It's sitting on the windowsill. I don't say nothing else to him. I just pull my straight razor outta my purse. He try to sit up then, try to raise his arm up to protect hisself, but I'm too quick. I try to slit that son of a bitch's throat. He look up at me surprised and start bleeding right away. His hand go to his neck, try to catch the blood. He choking, not gurgling. I don't think I cut him deep enough, but I don't stop to see for sure. I just get the fuck outta there.

Then I'm back at the bar looking for Margaret. She hugged up with that big dude in a back booth.

"Let's go," I say, catching hold of her arm and trying to hurry her along. "We gotta get outta here, now."

She try to shrug me off, saying, "Shoot, I'm having a good time. Why don't you come sit with us awhile?"

I drag her off to the side and tell her what's up. "I might a killed a man," I whisper. "We gotta go."

She look at me all bug-eyed and shit, but she go tell the big fella that we got to leave. He offer to drive us home, say his car is in the lot behind the bar. I say, "Good," and lead the way as we slip out the back door.

New Shoes

Last week, Belle came over to my house asking me to go downtown with her. I told her I didn't need nothing, but she come talking about, "Aw, Margaret, I don't want to go by myself. Come on. It'll be fun. Hudson's is putting up its Christmas displays." She know I like the decorations the big department stores put up this time of year. She saw I was about to give in so she rushed to keep me from coming up with another excuse.

"We'll be home way before the kids get home from school," she added.

I looked at my watch. It was early, so I figured we could get down there and back before school let out. So, we bundled up and headed out to the bus stop. It was snowing, but the flakes were light, the kind that melt when they hit your cheek. The temperature was maybe fifteen or twenty degrees, and the ground was hard with crusty patches of ice. Me, Belle, and her six-year-old son, George, but she call him Scooter, stood shivering next to the long metal pole with the tiny square sign that served as the bus stop. We was wrapped tight, scarves twisted around our faces and knit caps pulled down low on our heads. My coat was a little too short and my knees were red and stinging like somebody's momma had took a switch to them. Belle had this big ole black pocketbook hanging off her arm, and the wind kept knocking it hard against my frozen hip.

I felt really sorriest for Scooter cause he had on a pair of raggedy canvas gym shoes. Belle said she kept him outta school to buy him some winter boots. He kept stomping his feet to keep the blood going. White salty trails ran down his cocoa-colored cheeks. Belle popped him upside his head and told him to quit crying cause his tears was gon freeze, but that didn't stop him.

Finally, I saw the bus coming, but it was full. For a minute, I thought it might ride on past us, but it slowed and sloshed to a stop. The doors folded open, and Belle pushed Scooter up the steps. He stumbled, so she lifted him up by the collar and then the shoulders of his coat and shoved him up the rest of the way.

The bus jerked forward as we squeezed past old ladies with their knees curled around shopping bags, teenagers with book bags slung over their shoulders, and men in bulky coats and thick work boots. Belle found a empty slice of seat on one of the back benches. She jammed Scooter in, planted her feet in front of him, and grabbed a handrail. I slipped in next to her.

"First, we'll hit Hudson's basement," she said. "They got kids' shoes, and sometimes they have good deals. Then Kresge's; I need some stockings. Where did you want to go?" Before I could answer, she nudged me. "Look at that fool over there." She tilted her head toward a boy whose greasy hair was pushed up in the front to form a stiff black knob. A do-rag, spotted with oil, that looked like it had once been a nice scarf, was wrapped around his head. He looked straight ahead, as he slipped his hand into a woman's purse. She was standing beside him, smiling and looking out the window, anxious like she was eager to get where she was going.

Belle chuckled; I tucked my purse under my arm and turned to stare straight into a wrinkled brown face that had the hard eyes of a judge. A pinch of guilt made me turn away. Maybe I shoulda said something to the smiling lady, but sometimes these hoods carry knives or worse. The bus stopped short; I held the handrail tighter to keep from stumbling. A few men got off just as their connecting bus pulled up at the cross street. "Hold up!" one of the men shouted as he ran toward it, dodging cars.

The old man next to Scooter didn't miss a snore. His head bobbed up and down like he was listening to a blues beat, a line of spit slobbered down his chin. The smell of the cheap wine and the piss that stained his pants rose up and like a cloud of misery shoving its way into my face. I tried not to breathe.

A boy sporting a little Afro and wearing a green letterman jacket with a big white *C* had his arm hanging over his girlfriend's shoulder. His hand dangled just above her breast as her head leaned against his chest. Two more teenage girls sat just in front of them, their backs to the couple. The girl closest to the window was talking a mile a minute, hands making wild gestures. Her friend just nodded and twisted her lips like she'd heard it all before. They both had on neat little plaid pleated skirts, white blouses with Peter Pan collars, and camel-colored car coats with toggle buttons. I liked how clean and crisp they looked. I took a picture with my mind. When my girls get big enough, I want to dress them like that.

Belle nudged me again. "This our stop." She reached over the two girls to pull the bell. The one talking rolled her eyes, the other one looked at her friend and giggled. Belle didn't pay them no mind; she just grabbed Scooter's hand and dragged him along as she pushed through the crowd.

We scrambled across the crowded street to Hudson's. Belle lied. The window displays were still the regular ones, work dresses for office girls and business suits for men, no elves or sleigh bells in sight. We hurried past the expensive perfume counters and headed down the wooden escalator to the bargain basement. ✿

Scooter kept stopping every so often to stomp his feet. Somewhere along the way, he had latched onto a pair of Superman mittens. He kept putting them on and pulling them off. A mannequin wearing a long blue nightgown stood at the bottom of the wooden escalator, just off to the side. She stood on a pedestal looking down on us. The gown floated around her like silk and air; I had to touch it.

"Belle, feel this. It's so soft," I said.

She pulled at a piece of the hem and rubbed it between her thumb and forefinger. "It's just some kind of good polyester."

I looked at the price tag. "It should be silk for this kind of money."

But Belle had moved on. She was down the aisle looking at girdles in the underwear department. I hurried toward her, but I didn't need no girdle. So, I went to look at the underwire brassieres on the rack—way too expensive. I headed over to the cotton ones. When I turned around to look for Belle, she had a big shopping bag. I wondered what she had bought.

We went on down to the kids' shoe section, and this young white boy asked if he could help. Belle pointed to a couple different boots that he had on display, and he told us to sit in his section while he went into the back room to see if what she wanted was in stock.

Belle pulled off Scooter's wet shoes and socks. She squeezed the socks out, ignoring the dark stain it was making on the carpet. I couldn't help but laugh at Belle's nerve. I nudged her and nodded toward the pinched-faced white woman who stood behind the counter giving us the eye. Belle say she wasn't thinking about that ole heifer and went to rubbing Scooter's feet. The salesboy came back balancing a stack of boxes. Belle made him get Scooter a fresh pair of socks and then use that metal sliding thing to measure Scooter's feet. Then the salesboy was opening a box and pulling out a shiny new pair of cowboy boots. Scooter's eyes lit up.

He slid each boot over Scooter's fresh socks, and Scooter stood up, admiring his feet. Belle had him walk to the edge of the rug and then back again. She asked him how they felt. She bent down and pressed a finger to each toe to see where his foot sat in the boot. "Too tight," she announced. "Let's see those," she said, pointing to another box. But Belle had something negative to say about each pair. She had that white boy running back and forth to the storeroom. Scooter strutted around in tall boots that was "too tall," short boots that was "too low," and even a pair of "too shiny" pointy-toed ones. When all was said and done, the ones that looked and fit perfect was "too expensive." Scooter put back on his wet gym shoes, and Belle paid for the socks and took a free shoehorn.

We bundled up and headed cross the street to Kresge's. The store was really crowded, and since the makeup counter was the first one we came to, we checked out the new lipstick and fingernail polish colors. Belle said she was going upstairs to pick up some stockings. I didn't need none, so I went to the refreshment counter for a orangeade.

After that, I bought some thread cause I was planning on taking the hem outta my coat when I got home. When Belle came back downstairs, Scooter was right on her heels. I was looking at the jewelry. She handed me her shopping bag and said, "Hold this a minute for me." I took it, wondering what all she bought, cause that bag was heavy. I looked up to show her this necklace I liked and saw her and Scooter pushing through the revolving door.

At first, I didn't know what to think. Then I saw this big white man shouting something and hurrying in my direction. Everybody started looking at me. I near about peed on myself. My heart felt like a kettle drum, and the sweat from under my arms was soaking through my wool coat. The floorwalker, a skinny white man in a brown suit, turned his mean eyes on me. I stepped backward, toward the door. Then I remembered the shopping bag I was holding. It was so heavy the twisted paper handles bit into my wrist, making deep red gouges, and the bag strained, threatening to rip itself off its frayed handles. I let go of it, dropped it right there in the aisle between jewelry and makeup, and then I ran. There was shouting for a while, a man's voice, and people on the street looked scared as they scooted out of my way. But I just kept going, pushing past the ones that wouldn't move. I was way past Grand Circus Park before I even looked back.

That night Belle had the nerve to call me and ask if I still had her shopping bag. I asked was she a fool? She tried to explain that she had a police record and would have had to do some time, but since I didn't have one, I would have probably just got a warning or probation at the most. She talking about she didn't think the floorwalkers would pick up on me. According to Belle, that bag had Scooter's boots, the expensive ones, a Playtex long-line girdle and matching brassiere, some school dresses for our girls, and the blue nightgown I had been looking at.

"Right," I said. "You was thinking of me." I couldn't help but press my lips together and shake my head at her nerve.

"I was," she said, sounding like she meant it.

I don't know what Belle was thinking. I don't think she meant me any harm, and it was a shame about Scooter's boots, but that was the last time I ever went shopping with her. My friend Diane was always telling me I'm too gullible, that I could learn something from Belle cause she was a survivor, but that I shouldn't trust her as far as I could throw her. And Belle was no lightweight. Diane was right. I may be too trusting, but I ain't no fool, and I knew I had been lucky. I was just glad that that white man hadn't caught up with me, that I wasn't festering away in jail, and that I got to go on with my regular life.

The Crossroad

The church is full of Grandma; her long white box sits on a pedestal in the front. I can see her dark-brown face peeking out, the tip of her nose and a shiny chocolate cheek. There are lots of flowers, carnations with stiff pink bow ribbons. She liked carnations cause they last a long time. Roses, white and red, and loose-petaled yellow flowers are spread all around the box and across the stage circling the preacher's place. They smell pretty, sweet and fresh; I don't know where Momma is. I can't see her nowhere.

Wide, round, purple, blue, and black Sunday best hats nod, making soft waves that wash over rows of ladies in navy and black dresses. Every once in a while, there's a splash of green or deep purple or a man pressed tight in a dark suit and tie with a high-buttoned white shirt and brushed-back hair. An old, old lady with balled-up, brown-paper-bag skin is sitting across the aisle from us. She is wearing a wide navy hat with a big puffy, organdy flower pasted right on the front. She is humming a slow song that I can't make out. Her voice is rusty and wet.

I'm sitting on a bench scrunched between two church ladies wearing white uniforms. Crocheted doilies are pinned to the breast pockets of their crispy dresses. Pearl-like buttons go all the way down the front; only ankles in white stockings and thick-heeled shoes peek out. One of them keeps pressing my face against the crocheted doily on her pocket. It's stiff, not soft like it look. I try to wiggle my face away so I can breathe better, but the other church lady's bosom is guarding the other side. I stare down at the tiny white pearl-colored buttons on her wide white lap.

I have on new black patent leather T-strap shoes and my turquoise-blue dress with the long waist. Grandma called it my jazzy dress, said it looked like one she used to have when she was a girl. She showed me how to wear the long beads that came with it. When I tried the dress on in the store, Grandma took the necklace and put it around her neck. She wrapped it so that one part was close around her throat and the other hung down to her waist. Then she put one hand on her hip and pretended like she was chewing gum while she took the long part of the necklace in her other hand and twirled it around. She winked at me and said that's the way the fast girls did it. I laughed, and then she twirled the beads around again and made a cockeyed face. I laughed harder because she looked so funny. Then she picked me up and twirled me around. The beads feel smooth and bumpy. I smile.

I hear Momma somewhere crying. I turn to look for her, and she's there in the aisle held up by two ladies in white. Momma's face is red and crumbly, her mouth open wide, crying. Her friend Belle is coming up the aisle behind them. "*Diane*," she call out to Momma. Momma shake loose of the church ladies so she can hug Belle. Momma crying on Belle's shoulder. Belle hug her back. *Old sloe-eyed Deacon Harris*—that's what Grandma used to call him cause he was always trying to get with Momma—come up behind them and hand Momma his handkerchief. She take it and blow her nose. "*Diane. I got her,*" he say and try to take Momma from Belle, but Momma won't go.

"*I want my momma.*" I start crying. "*I want my momma.*" I'm standing on the wooden seat trying to climb over these church ladies, but they won't let me get to my momma. One of them is holding me by my waist, making me even more hot and sweaty, and this other lady is blocking my way. They won't let me get to my momma!

This lady saying, "*Baby come on sit down here with me. You can't have your momma right now.*" So I scream and cry and scream louder because I want my momma, and she right there and they won't let me have her. *Shh*, the lady in white croon in my ear. She try to rock me against the bumpy smoothness of her dress pocket as she wipe my nose with a handkerchief. *"Don't Sister Greene look good,"* my other keeper say. *"Swanson did a good job. Sister Greene would be real proud."* I peek out at Grandma, who is looking pretty and peaceful, and I quiet down because I know she would want me to.

"A good woman," say one of the church ladies, *"tithed 'til it hurt, and all those kids. She deserve a nice send-off."*

A crew of church lady nurses stand along the back wall, hands behind their backs, a line of straight white posts holding the church up. I'm wondering where they keep the cold rags and smelling salts they give the people who faint when they get the Holy Ghost.

Grandma would be standing there with them if she wasn't resting in her pretty box bed. Her hair is all shiny and curled like when she get it done on Saturdays. I smile and remember how Grandma used to say getting her hair done once a week was her one *indulgence.* A treat, she said it meant, like the little brown bag of penny Squirrels and Banana Splits she used to give me when she came home from the beauty parlor. Grandma was always teaching me new words and other things, like the capital of Colombia is Bogota. Colombia is a country way down south. She liked to read and tell me about other places. *Bogota.* I like the way the word sounds in my mouth.

Uncle Jeff is sitting up straight and crisp in his white Navy uniform. His face is quiet and serious; his mouth a straight line. He nod his head up and down every time Aunt Jamie whisper something in his ear, but he won't turn to look at her. Aunt Jamie look nice in the dark-blue suit she borrowed from Momma. Uncle Ronald is sitting next to her with some lady I don't know. Momma say every time she turn around Ronald got a new girlfriend. Uncle Ronald paint crazy pictures with weird mismatched colors. Momma say he can't see straight cause *he always high on that reefer*, but Grandma say he just trying to make sense out of this crazy world.

The organ music start, *Bringing in the sheaves, bringing in the sheaves. We shall come rejoicing, bringing in the sheaves.* The people in the choir stand up. One of my keepers take my hand, and we stand as we sing along with the choir. It sound good, full and loud, and I smile because Grandma is smiling. The preacher's black-and-purple robes swirl around him as he take his place in front of the tall stand that look like the thick trunk of a tree growing out of Grandma's box. *"We have come together this day to celebrate the life of this good woman, to rejoice in the fact that we were fortunate enough to have this gracious woman touch our lives. Let us begin with a prayer of benediction, a pronouncement of His divine blessing."* His words sound like a song as he bow his head and stretch his palm out to us.

We bow our heads too. I can feel Grandma's warm palm squeezing my hand, reminding me to be quiet, to bow my head and *let the gentle beauty of prayer wash over me.*

Diane's Daughter

I didn't want to be like her. I didn't want to be like Momma. I mean, I love her and I know she loves me, but there has to be more.

I met David at the Laundromat around the corner from our house. Momma had sent me over there to do the sheets and towels. He just came up and started helping me fold the sheets. He was such a gentleman, and so cute. Then he bought us a couple of pops, and we sat and talked while the towels dried. He wanted to carry the basket of clothes home for me, but I didn't want to have to explain him to Momma. After all, he had to be like twenty something. I was only sixteen, and I knew Momma would pitch a fit.

Anyway, he started coming around when Momma wasn't home. He'd call, and I'd let him in the back so the neighbors wouldn't see. It wasn't about sex or nothing; at least it didn't start out that way. David was just fun to be with, I liked listening to him talk, and we'd watch old movies on TV. We'd kiss and stuff, but he never pressured me to do anything more. In fact, it was me who suggested we go back to my room that first time, but of course, he got right into it. From then on, we'd watch TV while we snuggled up on a pallet of quilts in the living room. Sometimes he would bring me presents—a skirt and a blouse, or some colored underwear. I had to hide them in the bottom of my closet so Momma wouldn't find them. On days when he was busy and couldn't come over, I'd take them out and try them on.

The first time David picked me up from school, I didn't know who he was. He came riding up in this old-school blue Caddy, blowing his horn. Me and some of my friends were standing near the cornerstone talking. We ignored him because we figured he was just some old man trying to pick one of us up. Then he got out of the car. He looked good in his dark suit and baby-blue shirt with the collar open. He took off his shades, looked right at me, and called my name. I said bye to my friends and ran over to the car.

He started picking me up almost every other day after that. It was my junior year so I had an early program. I'd get out about two o'clock, and Momma would be on her way to work, so me and David would ride out to Belle Isle. He'd always have a cold bottle of wine, a couple of joints, and we'd stop and pick up some fried fish or some burgers along the way. He kept this old Indian blanket in his trunk. We'd find a shady spot under a tree and have us a picnic right on the bank of the Detroit River with the Windsor skyline just across the way looking like a postcard.

I thought he was cute, but he looked too young and was way too smooth for me. And anyway Verna let everybody know from the get-go that he was going to be hers. He wore dark sunglasses all the time, didn't even take 'em off in the bar. Maybe he wanted to hide what he was thinking, or maybe he didn't want nobody to see how red the weed made his eyes. When he was at the pool table or having a shot at the bar, the fellas would grin at him and say, "Hey cool!" or "You need to lighten up on the shades, man." But he would just laugh it off and take it as the friendly teasing it was. So we all just started calling him Shades. His shades had black squarish frames that matched his skin. And he always wore dark-blue, gray, or black tailor-made suits. He looked like a musician, one that would play moody jazz one minute and a crazy, spastic rhythm the next. When he talked, his voice had a low, pushy tempo like Mingus on bass when it got good to him, but Shades didn't talk much. With him it was like words was money, and he wasn't giving nothing away.

He didn't stand around in groups like some of the other men. If he was standing with another brother or two, it was quick, a few quiet words as something little passed between slapped hands. But mostly, he was by hisself slipping in an out of this or that bar, stopping to chat with the owner, or having a beer while he checked his watch and scoped out the place. You couldn't really tell how old he was because he kept those shades on all the time. But the skin on his face was tight and smooth, and his step was light and quick. Some folks said that the streets had been his home since he was ten and that he'd been dealing longer than that. You can't always believe what you hear, but from the way he carried hisself you could tell he'd been around awhile, and he was still young and good-looking enough to catch women's eyes.

Anyway, Verna let it be known that she wanted some of that "little black Negro." She was always smiling up in his face and talking about how she wouldn't even charge him for it. By that time, I didn't have the heart to compete with all the young girls crowding the block, and the streets were getting way too danger-ous. Even though I'd never really been one to work the streets, the few tricks I could still turn weren't enough to pay the bills so I got a job tending bar at Ernie's. Besides, Persia was coming of age and I had to set an example.

Verna and some of the girls used to come in to get warm in the winter, or for a cold one in the summer. For the most part, they treated me like I was they momma, sometimes asking ad-vice, but mostly just hoping I'd listen when they needed to talk. When they made good on the streets, they left good tips. And if it was tight out there, I'd give 'em a drink on Ernie. On nights when the bar was jumping, it was fun watching the girls flirting and acting crazy while the dudes tried to act like big shits.

Verna would put on a show whenever Shades came in. She would cross her legs and hike her skirt up extra high to give him a look at that long line of thigh. Then, it didn't matter who she was with, a possible trick or another one of the girls; she'd get to talking loud about how "dark men are so sexy" and how all they had to do was look at her to make her come. Most of the time, he would ignore her. He'd take care of his business and get the hell out of there. Verna would let out a belly laugh, and I'd shake my head at her nerve.

The first time Verna and Shades came in together, it shocked me shitless. When she came up to the bar to get their drinks, she looked up at me with bright eyes and a shit-eating grin on her face. Then she had the nerve to stick her tongue out at me. I just shook my head. Giggling like she'd been smoking weed, she switched her little ass back to the table. They sat back there awhile, him sipping his Bud and her talking and nibbling at the extra maraschino cherries I always gave her with her Champale grenadine. She was leaning all up in his face, and he was looking straight ahead like he was casing the joint. I wanted to tell her to quit throwing herself at that man, but I learned a long time ago to mind my own business when it came to things like that. Finally, he said something to her, and she got up and left. He went back by the pool table. Look like he was shaking hands with a couple of the fellas, but I knew what was going down. After that, he split.

From then on, he came in with Verna on a regular basis and later with other women. They'd talk, but he still didn't stay long, and he always made his trip back to the pool table. Verna was working through the week now, and she hardly ever came in to sit and talk with me. I missed her loud talk and crazy stories.

David had promised to pick me up from school, but he didn't show. I was glad I hadn't told my friends because I would have been embarrassed. I hung around school with them longer, and when I couldn't think of any more reasons to stall, we started walking home. I kept looking back hoping he was just late, but he never showed.

I didn't see him for about a week. He didn't call, but then one night he came scratching at my bedroom window. I was angry with him and decided to pout, but when I let him in he was all quiet, not at all like himself. So I got quiet too and waited. He took off his shoes and stretched out on the bed with all his clothes on. I went to turn on the radio, but he said, "Don't!" Then he patted a place on the bed next to him. I sat down and leaned against the headboard. He took off his shades, laid them on the table next to my bed, and rubbed his eyes. But he still didn't say anything, and I was getting tired of waiting.

So, I asked him where he'd been, and he said, "Trying to make some money."

"You could have called," I said, starting to fuss despite myself.

He shot back with, "Some of us have to make a living."

I wasn't used to him snapping at me like that. Checking himself, he slid up next to me and put his arm around me. I put my head on his chest and mumbled something about missing him.

"Don't mind me. I'm just uptight cause I been hustling hard and don't seem to be getting nowhere," he whispered as he smiled down at me.

I felt better as he rubbed my arm and started to talk.

"See I owe these people some money, and they don't believe in no payment plan." He laughed, "Sometimes, I wish I was a woman. They born with moneymakers." He touched my thigh, and we both laughed.

Then he turned to me like he just got the best idea in the world and started telling me how I could help him out of this situation. How it wouldn't even hurt me, probably do me some good, might even be fun. He spoke as he stroked my arm. At first, my feelings were hurt to think that he would want me to do it with somebody else, but he kept talking about how it wouldn't be for long, just until he got over the hump. He would show me what to do, and he'd always be there when I needed him. He promised he'd make it up to me if I just helped him out this once. Then, holding me tight, he told me how beautiful I was, that he'd never felt this close to anyone, and that one day he'd be able to give me anything I wanted. I told him I'd think about it. That seemed to make him happy. He kissed my forehead, my nose, both cheeks, then my lips. And as he made love to me, he breathed promises of our future together into my hair, ears, and neck.

Verna slid onto a barstool. She looked tired, and she wasn't smiling. I knew something had to be wrong because Verna always had a smile on her face. I fixed her a drink, and she showed a little teeth when I set the saucer of cherries next to her glass. She said thanks, and I went on down to the other end of the bar to take care of another customer. I laughed and joked a little bit with the man, rang up his drink, got my tip, and went back to putter around Verna. I could tell she wanted to talk. She was sipping her drink slow, and she hadn't touched her cherries.

She peeked up at me from under her false eyelashes and started to say something, but somebody pushed through the door, and she turned to see who it was. It was one of the regulars. He headed to the back room where a couple of other guys were playing pool. She looked relieved.

Then she leaned over and said, "I don't know how to say this, but I'm just gon let it out. David is turning your daughter out."

At first, I didn't understand what she was saying. It was like she was speaking Russian or some shit. My brain wouldn't take it in. I asked, "Who the fuck is David?"

She said, "You know, Shades."

I asked her how she knew, and she said, "He brought her to me for some pointers."

"Look," she said to me, "her name is Persia, right? She sixteen and go to Central, right?"

I was mad now; I asked her why she telling me this crazy shit. And she looked down at the floor and said, "Cause he spending too much time with her, and besides I thought you should know."

I asked Verna where Persia was right now. She said she didn't know because Shades had picked Persia up from the hotel a few minutes ago. Verna was hot because he had collected her earnings and rode off with Persia. Left Verna standing in front of the hotel without bus fare, told her to go earn it, checked her with a look when she asked if she could ride with them, and didn't say shit about where they was going or why.

I wanted to die right there; it hurt so bad. Instead, I went in the back to Ernie's office where he store the liquor and where he sometimes sit at a big wooden desk to read the paper. I told him I had to go, that he better get somebody to cover for me. Then I grabbed my purse and left him standing with part of the paper in his hand and his mouth open. Didn't even give him a chance to ask me why or if I was coming back.

When I got home, I headed straight to Persia's room, but she wasn't there. So I started looking through her stuff for a clue, a reason for her to do some crazy shit like this.

The Cinderella pencil case I bought her when she was about ten sat on top of her civics and English books, and below them was a neat stack of spiral notebooks. Next to them, on the top of the dresser, was a couple of bottles of fingernail polish, a bottle of remover, and a couple of emery boards. Underneath them was a clean white napkin. Some actor from one of those teen movies stared out from one wall, and tucked into a loose side of the poster was the dust jacket from some book called *A Wrinkle in Time*. I had to sit down on the bed cause for a minute my head started spinning and I couldn't breathe.

I started looking through her dresser, but I didn't find nothing but some EZ Widers and a little weed in a piece of tinfoil. I didn't get too upset cause I figure kids are bound to do a little experimenting, and if this was all the drugs she was doing, I was glad. Then I realized that Shades probably gave it to her. So I squeezed that tinfoil up tight as I could, tore the cigarette papers up into little pieces, and stashed 'em in the kitchen garbage under the bits of rotting tomatoes and potato peelings.

Frustration and anger tore at me, so I started throwing the stuff out of her closet, looking for what I didn't know. After a minute or so, I found a Hudson's shopping bag. It was packed all neat in the bottom of her closet behind her winter boots. I figured, this is it. I didn't know what, but I knew it was something. So, I took the bag and set down on the bed. I pulled out a couple of blouses that still had the tags on 'em. Then I dumped the whole bag out on the bed. A couple more skirts fell out, and then all this sexy-colored underwear tumbled out. At first,

I thought she had gone to stealing too. Then I saw these little note cards that they give you when you get a gift wrapped. They all said, "Love, David." I started tearing it all up; flimsy little brassieres and see-through blouses was flying everywhere. Then I just sat there and cried.

David parked his car a block over. We walked up the alley and tried the back entrance, but somebody had put on the chain lock. David said he would wait, but I figured it wouldn't matter just this once, so we went around to the front.

I felt really good. David had taken me riding over in Canada by Lake St. Clair. We rode way out past all these really big houses with yards for days, and then we just cruised awhile enjoying the lake and listening to the smooth jazz that David likes. I wanted to keep the mood as long as I could, so as soon as I got in the house I put on something slow and made David dance with me. He pursed his lips at me like I was being silly, and then he took me in his arms and started singing to me as we slow danced. That's when I saw Momma out of the corner of my eye.

At first, I didn't recognize her because she looked all shrunk up standing there in the dark. She was holding something, and she looked so sad, so strange, I didn't even think about her probably being mad cause David was there. I stopped dancing and called to her. "Momma?" But she didn't say anything, so I cut the light on so I could see what was wrong.

That seemed to do it because she just swelled up all of a sudden, and then she threw the bundle of clothes she had been holding in my face and started hollering.

I was about to make up something about David when I saw that she had thrown my colored underwear at me. Now she was pointing her finger in my face, asking me was I a fool loud enough for the folks that live down the block to hear. I looked to David, and she got real mad. Started screaming about how "that niggah better not say shit," I was her daughter and a minor. And if he didn't leave me alone, she was "gon have him put under the jail." Then she was hitting me upside my head. I ducked and landed on the floor, covering my head. I'm steady hollering, "Momma, what's wrong with you?" and she just hitting and cussing.

I started crying and wondered why he didn't pull her off me. Finally, she got tired and just plopped down on the floor next to me. I felt bad because I hurt her, but I was mad because she embarrassed me like that in front of David.

Then David said, "You don't have to stay here and take this shit. You can come with me and be treated like a woman."

Momma looked up at him. "Yeah, you can go make him some more money."

She looked at me and wiped some of the tears off my face.

"What he tell you, baby? That it's just for a little while? Just 'til you two get on your feet? I bet he didn't tell you about the other three girls he got working for him."

I looked up at David, and he shook his head sad-like. "She saying that shit cause she scared. Probably been scared her whole life. That's why she ain't got nothing and ain't never gon have nothing. You wanna be like her?"

"See baby, I been there." Momma kept talking. She was looking at me, right in my face, close. "Your daddy was just like this niggah. All street, pushing dope and dealing women. But I was in love, and I believed it was all for us. When I found out for myself that he was a selfish son of a bitch like that mothafuckah"—she pointed to David—"I picked you up from the babysitter's house and kept stepping."

"She just mad cause yo' daddy didn't come through for her. Just cause he wasn't shit don't mean all men like that. You know me. You know what I can do for you, what we can have together," he said, and then he held his hand out to me.

I didn't move. For some reason, I thought of that girl Verna standing in front of the hotel, looking miserable as we drove away. When I didn't take his hand, he licked his lips like they were dry, and then he let his hand fall back to his side.

But Momma kept talking, a rush of words like when she prays. "Babygirl, you got more in you than just making some mothafuckah's *car note. You smart, baby, and you can be something, something big. I know it. I know it." Momma was holding me and rocking me, and I was crying because something in me knew she spoke the truth and that she really loved me.*

David stood there looking down at us. He adjusted his shades using his finger to push them back up his nose, and then he shook his head like we disgusted him. "She just scared of losing you cause you all she got," he said. "If she could help it, you'd never have a life of your own. You got to love yourself enough to cut all this childish bullshit loose. You gon learn that everybody want something from you, even yo' momma. Being grown is learning to love yourself enough to say fuck any and everybody else, to say I'm gon take what I want, do what I want. Cause ain't nobody gon give you shit. You gotta be brave enough, strong enough to take it." He stood there like he was waiting for me to hear him, to understand. A part of me wanted to go to him. When he held me, I felt safe, but the way he stood there hovering over us like that was scary. Momma wiped another tear off my cheek. When I didn't move, he sighed and said, "You know where to find me." Then he turned and left, leaving the front door wide open. After a while I got up and closed it.

Please Love Me

He had her neck in the noose of his arm as she thrashed and struggled against him.

"What did I do, Willie?" Her voice was a pitiful whine.

When Paula first followed him out of the Tower, the Hamtramck burger joint where she worked, the crowd didn't pay much attention. She and Willie were always arguing. But when he grabbed her and wrapped his arm around her neck, their mouths fell open. Willie wasn't one to hit a woman; he'd shout, maybe threaten, but in the end he'd turn his back on her and walk away. It was always Paula who did the grabbing, the swatting, the following; her toes at his heels as her words scorched his neck. He was one of the good ones. But even through the window, they could see his black calloused hand raised. It landed hard, and her cheek reddened. And then he was grabbing her, his dark fingers pressing into the soft white flesh. She thrashed around at first, calling him a cocksucker and a fucking nigger while kicking at him, but he held on. After a minute or so, she must have gotten tired or was taking a minute to figure out a better strategy because she stopped resisting.

Eyes like an abused puppy, she looked up at him and wailed, "I love you."

They were white, most of the men who worked with Willie. They helped him hoist bulky steel doors onto the frames of new cars; they waited in line with him at the lunch wagon in front of the factory. They were the same guys that dropped by the Tower for a cup of coffee after work and sat at the counter complaining about long hours and aching joints. Now they stood red-faced, mouths hanging open, unable to breathe as he grabbed her by her hair. Strings of platinum spilled over Willie's big black fist, and she spoke of love.

Paula was a big girl, probably outweighed Willie by more than thirty pounds. Like many of the younger people who lived in the hamlet of Hamtramck, she was the second generation of her family to be born in the US. Her parents, grandparents, and most of the men who frequented the Tower were the sons and daughters of Polish immigrants, proud and sturdy.

Now she was half kneeling in the gutter, letting that *murzyn* put his hands in her face. She reached up to him, a supplicant, but he batted her hands away, and at one point his hands found her neck, thick black finger circling the white column. Struggling against him, scratching at his arms and barely able to breathe, she managed to ask him why he didn't love her. Nostrils flaring, he closed his eyes, and the growl on his face slid off. He shook his head, and after a few seconds, he released her.

She slid into the gutter, which was drying after an early morning rain. The slightly damp leaves and muddy slime were clumped cakes and smears. So it wasn't too slippery when she rose to her knees. Trembling, but steady, she knelt there, reaching up, pulling at his arms, tugging at the legs of his pants, her dirt-encrusted fingers grabbing, trying to catch hold of some part of him, any part of him. And then he kicked her, hard, in the stomach.

"You used to love me," she said. "Why don't you love me anymore?"

"Just stop!" he spit out.

"Please love me," she cried.

The men in front of the Tower saw and heard it all. Some, old and well into retirement, were huddled into thick sweaters. Others still wore work clothes, the greasy blue jeans and plaid flannel shirts that smelled of machine oil and sweat. The younger ones, whose bodies had been honed by hoisting windshields and bending to the urgent pace of the line as they greased doorjambs and polished headlights, tensed and leaned forward, ready to spring. Torn between disgust, anger, and allegiance to race and sex, they hovered in a frozen lunge like stone men in a life-sized relief. Frozen, they watched as Willie's booted foot left a dirty print on the crisp white of her waitress uniform. Paula, who always had a joke or a smile when she refilled their coffee cups, sat bowed in the mud of the gutter. Eyes snarling, mouths tight, and fists balled, they stood watching, and the urge to spring caused the blood to rush up their necks and stain their faces. And then they heard the words as she begged, "Please love me."

They grimaced en masse as the contents of their stomachs pushed up toward their constricting throats, and they looked away. Their eyes darted toward the gleaming windows of Margolis Furniture across the street, searched passing cars, scanned the cracked mud that lined the gutter, and assessed their work boots. Anything but witness this thing that was not happening.

Then two uniformed, hulking, red-faced Hamtramck cops, each over six feet tall, came out of nowhere. A squad car, the bar of lights attached to its roof flashing red, blocked the street. But it couldn't distract from what was going on in the gutter. The cops grabbed Willie, one on either side. He sighed and then bent over to receive the pounding blows of their batons.

All of a sudden, Paula was pulling at the policemen, shouting for them to leave Willie alone. One of the cops shoved her, and she fell back into the nearly dry dust of the gutter. Before she could get up, they had dragged Willie to the car, pushed him into the back seat, and slammed the door. Sirens blasting, they sped away. Flashing red lights scored her face as she stood in the middle of the street screaming, "He didn't do anything. It was my fault." Then she turned to the Tower's customers who still stood watching and said, "Those pigs better not hurt Willie."

After that, she seemed to wilt, and head down she waded back toward the Tower. No one touched her; no one tried to comfort her. Her tears had turned the dust to mud, and long, grimy streaks striped her face; she batted at them with the back of her hand.

Cassandra, one of two waitresses who'd just come on duty and the only black woman in the crowd, stood hugging herself, fingers clutching her upper arms as she watched Paula dust and straighten her skirt. A gust of wind blew Cassandra's apron up around her breasts. Paula's crumpled face turned toward her, and Cassandra knew Paula wanted a hug, some sympathy, but she just couldn't give it. A chill ran down her back, and her fingers made dents in the soft flesh of her upper arms. She didn't know what she felt. She wasn't mad, and it certainly wasn't funny, but she wasn't sympathetic either. So she looked away from Paula as she adjusted her apron and went back into the restaurant and took her place behind the counter.

A few of the older men from the crowd followed her back into the Tower. Each slid silently onto a stool facing the counter or sat at a table near the window, refusing to look at each other. After a few minutes, someone mumbled, "Coffee," and the others followed suit. Cassandra grabbed the nearly full pot off the burner, served each of the customers, and then poured a short one for herself.

Marie, an older Polish woman who was working with Cassandra that night, didn't move. She kept sitting on her stool, filterless cigarette poised between skinny fingers, as she sipped her Stanback-laced black coffee. She hadn't come outside, but she'd watched everything from the long plate glass window that ran along the front of the restaurant.

"Can I come in and get cleaned up?" Paula asked. Her shift had long since ended, but she stood at the door that led to the back room storage space with its employee bathroom and the narrow work space behind the counter. She wasn't crying anymore, but her face was red and mud streaked. Cassandra unlocked the door.

Cassandra and Paula had gone to high school together, but Paula ran with girls who wore false eyelashes, layers of pale lipstick, and smoked weed in the bathroom. Every now and then, Cassandra might hit a joint and tell Paula what she missed in class. And once, when Cassandra was on the bus sitting alone in the back, Paula left her friends to come and ask how she'd done on a quiz.

They were in junior year when Paula asked if Cassandra could get her a job at the Tower. Turnover was pretty quick so the guy that owned the place was always looking for someone. Waitresses had to shelve stock, mop floors, serve, work the register, and sometimes cook for less than minimum wage. The customers liked Paula because she was eager to please, and tips were always better when Paula was on shift. The other waitresses liked her because she was willing to split tips and do the dirtier jobs like cleaning the bathroom or the grill.

Paula dated a few of the younger guys from the neighborhood. It never lasted long, and they spread the word that she was easy. Once that got around, most every guy under sixty and a couple over tried talking her up to see what they could get. She wasn't into old guys, and for some reason she seemed to slow down. After the freshness wore off, they stopped asking and she became a fixture around the place.

Herb was the first black guy she dated. He came in every night after his shift, had coffee and a burger, and left a decent tip. He was friendly enough, but everyone was still surprised when she started going out with him. Big and raven skinned, he had an ample belly and a lisp. Besides, he was at least fifteen years older than Paula, and he was married.

She would meet Herb at the Tower, and they would go out for a drink or to the drive-in and then to a motel. After a while, Herb complained that it was hard for him to sneak a change of clothes out of the house. So they'd just have a burger at the Tower and then go to the motel.

Willie was muscular, had a flat stomach and no lisp; he was much more attractive than his friend Herb. They worked together, Herb on the line and Willie in the foundry. After Willie and his wife separated, he started eating most of his meals at the

Tower. Sometimes he'd meet Herb and Paula there, and they would all go to a bar together. But from the beginning, Paula seemed drawn to Willie. Like a moth to a streetlight, she fluttered to his side whenever he came in. Even when she was with Herb, she'd lean across the table grinning at Willie and touching his arm or his knee.

One night at the Tower, Willie confessed to Herb that he'd been sleeping with Paula. "You said she was just a fuck. You said she didn't mean nothing to you," he offered as an excuse. But Herb wasn't having it; he reared back and knocked Willie off the stool, and then he left, pulling open the heavy door all wild like he wanted to rip it off its hinges. He meant for it to slam and make a satisfyingly loud noise, but it only sucked hard at the air when it closed because it was weighted and made to take abuse.

Willie got up, dusted himself off, and went to meet Paula, who was waiting for him in the little room he'd been renting since separating from his wife. Herb stayed away from the Tower for a time, but eventually he was back ordering his usual half-raw burgers and coffee. At first, he wouldn't give his order to Paula, but after a while it was as though they'd never been a thing.

A beaming Paula couldn't say enough about how good Willie was to her, how he took her to the State Fair, to the movies, instead of drive-ins, and once to eat at a classy restaurant downtown called the Top of the Flame. Paula, who never called in sick and was always willing to take somebody else's shift when they needed a day off, started taking days off work. Whenever they came into the Tower, she would cling to him like he was a life-sized teddy bear she'd won at a carnival. She couldn't stop grinning. But then he started seeing his wife again, and Paula stopped smiling. Her anger spilled out like dirty mop water sloshing out of a toppled bucket.

"That black bitch better leave my man alone." The words came out loud and ugly like she'd forgotten she was in mixed company. But before Cassandra could say anything, Paula caught herself. "You know I don't mean anything by it. It's just that I really love Willie, and now that woman is trying to get him back." Cassandra smirked, and although she let it slide that time, the damage was done.

Instead of taking time off to go out with Willie, Paula started working extra hours again, but when she was at work she'd mope and complain. "He says he's going to see his kids, but he's probably somewhere fucking that bitch," she'd confide to Cassandra. A couple of times she slipped. "That *nigger* is just full of lies," she said once. And then, as she realized what she'd said, her face took on an oops look, and she said, "You know this is not about race. He just makes me so mad."

Paula decided to talk to his wife. She went to the Tower before heading over to *that woman's* house because she wanted to talk it out with Cassandra, who, after hearing her plan, told her that it wasn't a good idea and asked her what she thought it would accomplish. "I just want to tell her that I really love Willie and that she should leave him alone," she cried. "It would probably do more harm than good," Cassandra told her. But Paula went anyway.

Willie's wife invited her in and listened to what she had to say before holding the door open and asking her to leave. But Willie, who was coming up the walkway just as she was leaving, yanked Paula by the arm and told her that he would kick the shit out of her white ass if she ever came around his wife again. Paula went back up to the Tower crying, asking Cassandra what she should do. Cassandra told her to leave it alone. "He told you he didn't want to be bothered," she warned her. "He picked, and it wasn't you. You should listen to him." But Paula felt like she could change his mind.

She kept sneaking around his place, waiting for him on the front porch of the house where he'd rented his room, calling him in the middle of the night, and calling the Tower to see if he was there. A couple of times she even called his wife's house, telling her that she knew he was there and demanding that his wife put him on the phone.

He couldn't even get a hamburger to go without her coming around the counter and trying to drag him into a corner and drowning him with, "Willie, I want to talk to you . . . Willie, you can't just do me like this, you can't just . . . You said you loved me . . . Why are you acting like this . . . Willie . . ." She gnawed and yanked at him in front of the men he worked with, in front of the boys she'd slept with before him, in front of the women who worked at the Tower, and in front of Herb, who was his buddy again. So one day he just said, "Bitch, you better leave me alone."

He stormed out of the Tower, pulling wildly at the chrome bar of the heavy glass door, like he wanted to rip it off its hinges. It would have slammed really loud, but it only sucked hard at the air because it was weighted and made to take continuous use and abuse. Paula followed him out to the curb, saying, "Willie, you can't just treat me like this . . ." and he punched her in the face and grabbed her by the neck.

Now she was in the back washing her face, and Willie was probably in a holding cell down at the precinct. Paula came out of the restroom looking a little better; her face was clean, and she had used a damp dish towel to dust most of the dirt off her uniform, leaving only tiny damp smears.

"You think I should go down and bail him out?" she asked Cassandra.

"Maybe you should let his wife do it," Cassandra said, leaning against the doorjamb of the arch that led to the narrow walkway behind the counter. Marie was standing over the grill, pressing a burger with the metal spatula. "Maybe you should just leave him alone," Cassandra added, crossing her arms over her breasts.

"I just . . . ," Paula said and then stopped to keep the tears from falling.

Cassandra nodded and said, "I know, but sometimes you just have to love yourself more."

Paula's face was shiny with tears, and Cassandra could tell she wanted to be held, but Cassandra just couldn't. So she said, "See you tomorrow," as she pushed off the doorjamb and went to unlock the back room door. "Yeah, tomorrow," Paula said as Cassandra gave her shoulder a quick pat and rub. She gave Cassandra a watery nod in return and then made her way past the customers and pulled the heavy glass front door open. The door, built to take continuous use, sucked hard at the air and closed with a quiet shush behind her. Head down, she walked past the long plate glass window and down the block, heading home.

Mr. Phil

Phil's forgotten Kool collected a long, thin ash on the waist-high window ledge. He had both hands in his pockets, his right thumb and forefinger absently rubbing the smooth steel and plastic of his General Motors key ring.

"I remember a time when a nigger would have been afraid to do something like that to a white woman." He spoke in a slow, angry whisper.

"Yeah," Andy, another old-timer, agreed, shaking his head over the thick White Tower mug and feeling the steam from the hot black liquid on his face. Andy was Phil's best buddy. They'd known each other more than fifty years, ever since Andy moved up here from Kentucky. He had been a Kleagle with the Klan, and had recruited Phil back in '38. He planted his feet on the greasy black-and-white tile floor and twisted his stool around to face Phil, who stood leaning with his back to the wide plate of glass that looked out onto the busy Joseph Campau thoroughfare.

"We'd a took care a him." Andy smiled over at Phil, who looked away. "They'd a had to scrape him off the tracks once the 9:10 to Chicago made its run." He slapped his knee. "Member how them niggers was always losing their way over on them tracks down by Caniff?" He guffawed and slapped his knee again. "Got to be a epidemic for a while." Andy grinned at Phil, who looked up at the clock over the pastry shelves, then turned back toward the window.

Andy leaned forward. "Member that summer of '43 when the niggers decided to act up cause some little pickaninny or other got itself kilt out on Belle Isle?" He waited, and when he got no response, he went on. "Member? We had a strong klavern then. Ernie Dean was the Grand Cyclops. Good ole Ernie Dean, died a couple of years ago. Cancer, I think." He stood up and went to stand next to Phil so he could keep the conversation between the two of them. His words held some of the old excitement as he talked to Phil's ear in a low voice.

"Ernie called that emergency meeting. There was nearly seventy-five men that came, a lot of 'em father and son. Young men were more responsible then." He nudged Phil to encourage a nod of agreement. Phil continued to look up the street.

"Member Ernie pounding that lectern with his fist? 'These niggers is got outta hand,' he says. 'They's looting down in Paradise Valley. Tearing up they part a town is OK, but we cain't let 'em spill over down this a way.' Then he went to organizing patrols. Me, you, Jim, and Cozy got this side of town. Member you had the Buick? Smooth riding car. Roomy."

"Was a good car," Phil agreed.

"Then they shot one of the boys in the North End patrol. Think it was Ernie's son-in-law. Young boy, no more than twenty-one or two."

"Those boys went looking for trouble. Riding through the colored neighborhoods. Car full of boys drinking, cussing and calling people names. Niggers said they was throwing beer bottles at their windows and harassing their women."

"A little roughhousing's no reason to shoot a man dead."

"Look what we did."

"An eye for an eye. Had to teach 'em a lesson, or they'd a thought they could just kill a white man any ole time."

"But what about that man coming out of that movie house downtown? And his lady friend?"

"Boys had just got a little carried away by then. Smelled blood, you know."

"The man, alright. But . . ."

"It was Cozy that lit her skirt; and then the fire just went its own way. Thangs got outta hand."

Phil was shaking his head slowly, his eyes on the passing cars.

"He probably just meant to scorch her a little." Andy chuckled at his own joke. "You gotta admit the niggers acted right for a long time after that."

Phil could see Belle coming toward the Tower. She was wearing her White Tower uniform, but her green apron was draped across her forearm. Smiling, she spoke to every passerby. Each returned the greeting. As she passed the window, she smiled and waved at him. He noted how black her skin was in contrast to the white uniform. When she pushed through the door, it emitted a gust of hot air. She stood just inside the door, mopping her forehead with the back of her hand. Andy was silent now; he moved toward the counter and pushed his cup toward Marie, indicating that he wanted a refill. Phil watched Belle as her body seemed to relax in the air conditioning.

"God, it's hot out there," she breathed.

He smiled at the smooth shininess of her skin and the way the roundness in the back of her skirt swayed as she made her way to the door that led to the storeroom and the back of the counter.

Belle stood in the open door, surveyed the room, pressed her lips together, and made a smacking sound of disapproval as she eyed the floor. Marie leaned farther over the grill and pretended to scrape at a dark smear of grease.

"One of y'all should've mopped this floor. It's filthy." Belle spoke to Marie as she tied on her apron.

"Lillian left early, and I been here by myself for the last three hours," Marie offered, not looking back at Belle, who was pulling the heavy mop bucket out.

"If a customer had slipped on that grease out there, Mr. Norris a give you hell."

"Well, he should supply some more reliable help. I had to work the whole lunch hour by myself."

"Marie, this is Sunday. Ain't even no lunch hour to speak of. Sides, you always trying to get out a mopping this floor." Belle rolled the bucket under the spigot, poured the soap powder in liberally, and filled the bucket with hot, sudsy water. As she began to dunk the mop in and out of the bucket, Marie scooted past her.

"I don't know who you think you are. Your lily-white hands getting paid the same as mine."

Marie didn't say anything else. She just pulled her pocketbook off the shelf, tucked it under her arm as she signed out. Then she unlocked the back door, leaving it slightly ajar as she headed toward the exit. Phil, seeing his opportunity, pulled the door open just as Belle was pushing the heavy bucket out onto the tile floor.

"Need some help with that?" he offered, bending toward the bucket. Belle smiled down at Phil, who was a small man, probably always had been, but old age was eating at his bones and shrinking him up more. She shook her head and sort of chuckled.

"Naw, I can handle it. But thanks."

Phil beamed up at her and then took a stool at the counter, making sure that his feet were safely up on the foot bar and out of her way.

Phil had treated Andy to a meal at Under the Eagle, a real sit-down restaurant, the best Hamtramck had to offer. After they ate, they'd had a drink over at the Polski Bar across the street from the Tower. But nine o'clock had come and gone, and Phil knew that the girls at the Tower changed shifts at ten. So, he left Andy at the bar with a fresh beer and headed across the street.

Belle was still on by herself. He watched her put two meat patties on the grill for a teenage couple who were sipping Cokes at the far end of the counter. A black man about forty stood by the jukebox reading the record titles and picking his teeth with a toothpick. Phil slid onto a stool and waited for Belle to pay attention to him. She flipped the burgers over, pressed them a couple of times with the metal spatula, lifted a couple of handfuls of frozen fries into the fry basket, and lowered the basket into boiling grease. Then she came over to where Phil sat.

"What you need?" she asked as she rinsed dishes in the sink just below the counter.

"Coffee," Phil said almost inaudibly. Then he nodded to the black man near the jukebox. "Friend of yours?"

"Why?"

"Just curious."

"Just a customer," she said, wiping her hands on her apron. "Said he works at Kowalski's."

She shook out a freshly washed cup, poured the hot black liquid into it, and then slid it across the counter so that it stood in front of him.

"I was just wondering if maybe you had time for a drink when you get off," he asked, avoiding her eyes.

"That's real nice of you, but my feet are killing me after eight hours on this concrete, and I gotta go out there and wait on that slow-ass Sunday Holbrook bus."

"Well, I could give you a ride home. You know, my room is only a couple blocks away. I could go get the T-bird, and I got a fifth of Black & White. We could have a little sip in the car before I take you home."

Belle looked at the little old man and smiled.

"OK," she said. Then, looking at the clock, "You better get going. I get off in bout twenty minutes."

Phil hopped off his stool, pulled a dollar off the wad of bills he kept in his shirt pocket, slid it across the counter, and headed toward the exit.

"Be back in ten minutes," he said to the back of the black man's head as he passed the jukebox.

Belle held the half-filled Styrofoam cup. She swished the gold-colored liquid back and forth over the ice cubes to give it a chill. Phil leaned back against the leather headrest of the T-bird's bucket seat listening to the river lap against the beach and watching the necklace of light that outlined the Ambassador Bridge. After a while, he put his Styrofoam cup on the dashboard, pulled his pack of Kools out of his shirt pocket, and offered Belle one.

"Too sweet for me," she said, searching in her purse for the Pall Malls. "I like to taste the tobacco." She pulled a cigarette from her pack as Phil held his lighter out to her.

"Thanks," she said, dropping the pack back into her purse and leaning toward the fire.

"This is nice." She sat back, enjoying the smell of the leather upholstery and the occasional breeze from the river. "You had a good idea to come out here. This is the first time I been to Belle Isle this year. Ain't had no time, what with working six days. I don't usually feel like going nowhere on my one off day.

"Phil," Belle asked tentatively, "I don't mean to get into your business, but I was just wondering how you make a living?"

"I'm retired."

"But how can you afford this car, and you be paying for Andy and them other men friends of yours when they short. And you always leave a good tip." She blessed him with a smile. He took a sip from his cup to hide his pleasure.

"When I was younger, I had a pretty decent job. I worked at Burroughs. It was a new company when I started work there. They used to give stock in the company as a sort of incentive, to encourage loyalty among the employees. Well, anyway, I retired with a pretty good pension, and the stock pays decent dividends. Besides, my wife died a few years back, and my kids are all grown and doing OK. I don't have much else to spend my money on . . . How about you?"

"How about me what?"

"Your family. Is there someone special in your life?"

"Well, yeah, I got kids, and I always have me a man. Before Carlos—that's my husband—before he left the last time, I had men after me. And when I knew he was gone for sure, I just picked one of 'em. I always had a man staying with me, more for finance reasons than anything else. Michael is my *squeeze* now." She giggled; the old word sounded funny, and the liquor was starting to work. "We been together a couple years now. We get along pretty good. He work at Chrysler, and he help me out most times. I can't complain."

Phil sipped his drink and thought about what she had said. "Is he a jealous man?"

At this she laughed outright. "Mister Phil, what you trying to say? We just out here shooting the bull and having a drink. You thinking about giving Michael cause to be jealous?"

"Well, I was just wondering if you ever, maybe, have a little time for somebody else."

"I honestly don't have much time for that kind of stuff anymore, but Michael ain't a violent man. That's one of the reasons I like him . . . But Phil, you got to understand that you and me can be friends—that's all."

"I wouldn't take much of your time, Belle," Phil said, putting his hand on her knee.

She didn't flinch or move away. She was quiet, as though she was thinking about him, about his words. Then slowly she smashed her cigarette out in the ashtray that lay open on the dashboard between them. Then she placed her palm on top of the spotted white hand that rested on her knee.

"Look. I used to be kinda wild when I was young, but those days are gone. I'm a church-going woman now; I got me a pretty good man, and a steady paying job. I really just don't want to complicate my life no more. Like I said, we can be friends. We can have a drink from time to time. I really appreciate you giving me a ride home tonight, but anyway, I just figured you a nice guy."

Phil stared at the trees that allowed him only a patchy view of the river. Then he took another sip from his cup, and they sat like that for a while, quietly sipping and watching the river through the trees.

From then on, Belle just accepted Phil into her life. He did her little favors, and she gave him company and conversation. Most days he'd pick her up from home and take her to work. When it was about time for her to get off, he'd just show up, his sleek tan Thunderbird parked outside. He'd always have a pint of Black & White and a couple of Styrofoam cups ready for the drive home. Most days, Belle would climb in, take her shoes off, and pour as he took the route back to her place. Occasionally, Michael would come to pick her up, and Phil would stand at his post by the window sucking on a Kool as Belle slid into Michael's Mercury sedan, but that wasn't too often because Michael was usually at work when Belle got off.

Whenever Phil went to Belle's house to pick her up for work, kids were always sitting on the porch, playing hopscotch or running relays on the front walk. At first the noise and movement intimidated him, but he liked their spirit, the sheer joy and freedom. The first time he came to pick Belle up, the kids stopped playing and peered at him cautiously. He'd gotten out of the car and was making his way to her flat when a boy who looked to be about fourteen ran to an open window on the porch and shouted, "Momma, it's some white man in a brown-on-brown T-bird here to see you." Belle came to the window and waved at him.

"Hey, Phil." She smiled that smile. "Give me a minute." And then she was gone. Phil backtracked and was leaning against the car waiting for her when a group of about four or five kids ranging in age from five to fifteen crowded around him and the car.

"Man, that's a nice car," they chorused.

A boy about ten years old ran his fingers along the freshly washed hood.

"Can I sit in it?" he asked.

Phil opened the door, and the kid slid in. Before long, the car was full of kids demanding turns at sitting behind the wheel, climbing onto the camel-colored bucket seats, and spinning the steering wheel making screeching noises. By the time Belle arrived, they'd begun to blow the horn and twist the knobs of the radio.

"Y'all know y'all better than that. Get your asses out that car." The words were spoken softly, but with a fierceness that promised immediate retribution, and suddenly the car was empty, the doors snapping shut and the swarm of bodies retreating to the porch.

After that, the visits weren't as eventful. He'd pull up, and before he could get out there'd be a chorus of "Mister Phil here." Once in a while, he'd get a chance to go in and sit on the sofa while he waited for Belle. Other times, she'd be headed out of the door before he could make it up the porch stairs.

On her off days, Phil turned up like clockwork, every afternoon at four. She'd be cooking dinner, and he'd come scratching at her door with a brown paper bag in his hand. He usually brought a six-pack, chips, or maybe some cookies for the kids, paper cups, and his trusty bottle of Black & White. Once the door was open, he'd head straight to the kitchen, plop down in one of the raggedy vinyl dinette chairs, and start setting up.

At first, Michael got mad when he'd see "that ole white man" sitting at the kitchen table. If Phil was there when he got home, he'd let the screen door slap real hard, grunt something at Belle, then he'd throw a nasty look at the little old man who sat bent over the shaky Formica table. Phil would stare into his can of beer or his cup of whiskey like he had done something wrong and Michael had caught him out. If Michael greeted him, he returned it, but usually he stayed silent, and Michael would kiss Belle on the cheek and head upstairs to take his bath.

He wouldn't come back down, even for dinner, as long as Phil was there. When Belle took Michael his dinner, he would ask in a loud voice, "When that ole fart gon leave?" Then he would try to pull Belle down on the bed, kissing her on her neck and touching her sensitive spots, so she would have to leave Phil downstairs by himself. Sometimes she would let Michael have his way, but on those occasions, she would have already fixed Phil's plate and left him eating with the kids. That way, she figured she kept everybody happy.

When her middle daughter, Celestine, got a scholarship to State, it was Phil who drove Belle up to Lansing so she could check on her and take her care packages; an hour and a half drive that took the old man three. His frail body fit so far down in the seat that he looked like a little boy peering over the steering wheel. The state troopers must have been able to tell he was an adult by the wispy white hair that stuck up over the steering wheel because they never stopped him. Besides, he kept way over in the slow lane and with a concentrated effort hovered around the required minimum of forty-five miles per hour. He didn't seem to notice the other cars whizzing by. He just kept his eyes straight ahead and talked happily to Belle, encouraging her to tell stories or find something she wanted to hear on the radio.

Celestine always waited for them on the front steps of her dorm with her lips poked out in disgust. She'd greet them hurriedly, then rush them upstairs. She didn't like for her friends to see her mother coming to visit her with "a squeezed-up old white man who could barely see over the steering wheel and who walked as slow as he drove." But in the confines of her dorm room she eagerly accepted the twenty-dollar bills he slipped her "to help out with books," along with the baked goods and fresh fried pork chop sandwiches her mother had brought her. In her room, she'd hug and kiss them both, expressing unrestrained gratitude. Sometimes the gifts would put her in a generous mood, and if the campus wasn't too crowded or if her mother insisted, she'd take them on a brief tour.

As time wore on, Phil became irritable during the drive up. He began to curse the "crazy youngsters" that whizzed by him, but Belle would soothe and cajole him all the way. And he was always better by the time they pulled up in front of the dorm.

Then he started forgetting he'd paid for a meal, or he'd swear he'd given the waitress a twenty when it was a five. A couple of times, in the dead of winter, he forgot to put on his socks. He'd forget names too, not just passing acquaintances but the person he'd been talking to and what they'd been talking about. But it was worse when he was driving. He'd drive no more than twenty miles an hour at all times, and he'd never take the freeways. It got so that Belle's kids didn't want him taking them anywhere. They'd laugh and say, "I'll race you." Then they'd start walking and moving in slow motion like a turtle or a movie that had slipped off its track. Belle and his friends at the Tower took it in stride. They didn't ask for any more rides, and they were patient with him when he got all in a huff about being served coffee when he ordered orange juice or when it was his turn to pick up the newspapers for the old guys and he'd come in empty-handed. They just ignored his outraged cursing or accepted his lame excuses.

But Phil knew something was wrong. His mind, his memory, wandered in and out, and it made him angry so he usually took it out on the first person he saw once his thoughts jiggled back into place. Sometimes when he was driving, he'd stop for a light, and suddenly the honking of the cars behind him would startle him. He'd get to fumbling with the gears in order to get the car going, but more and more often one of them would speed alongside, passing his car and shouting rude remarks. "It ought to be illegal for dead people to get a license to drive," one young man hollered as he gunned the motor. "There should be a breathalyzer for senility," another yelled. Too often, as they sped carelessly around, they'd just miss scraping the finish off his T-bird, and he'd shake an angry fist at them as he tried to swerve out of their way. Sometimes, and it was beginning to happen more often, he or the oncoming car would have to swerve out of the way because he had wandered out of his lane.

He made up his mind that he had to be more careful, maybe drive more slowly, maybe have a cup of coffee before he had to drive so he'd be more alert, but he just couldn't give up his T-bird. That would mean that he wouldn't be able to go over to Belle's for dinner or a drink, or just to watch her move around her kitchen. He did not want to do without the sound of that deeply Southern voice. It tickled him the way she scolded her children, and he especially liked it when she sang some popular tune that had gotten stuck in her head because it had been played so many times by one of her love-struck teenagers.

Without the T-bird, he'd have to miss out on his occasional drive to the suburbs to visit his grandchildren or his son or daughter, who never came into the city because there was "too much crime" or, as his son often said, "because everything we could ever need is right here." So, Phil kept his T-bird because giving it up would mean giving up everything he enjoyed about living.

He had his fourth minor accident coming from the eye clinic where he'd gone to insist on having his prescription strengthened. At the scene, he'd climbed carefully out of the car, his brittle body moving slowly. Finally, he confronted the other driver, a young woman whose toddler gazed curiously at him from the window of the driver's seat.

The woman, incensed, was shouting toward a gathering crowd, "I don't believe this. What could he have been looking at? Did you see how he came out of nowhere?" Then, to Phil, "Don't you know that this is a two-way street?" Embarrassed, Phil couldn't look directly at her. Then, mustering his courage, he searched her face for a little compassion and whispered apologies. "You're bleeding," she screamed. "Somebody call an ambulance."

This incident brought his son in from the suburbs, got his insurance canceled, and though his injuries were superficial, he ended up in the hospital enduring a series of tests.

Belle went to see him as soon as she found out. That day his daughter-in-law, bearing a small terrarium with a sand base, decided to make her obligatory visit. Belle was leaning over the top of his bed and fluffing his pillow. She was recounting a recent baseball game in which two of her sons had starred when the well-dressed middle-aged white woman appeared at the foot of his bed.

She smiled down at Phil. "Well, who is your friend, Poppa?"

"This is Belle. Belle, this is Elaine, my son's wife."

Belle, smiling, extended her hand toward Elaine, who touched the tips of her fingers briefly, then turned back to Phil.

"How've they been treating you, Poppa?"

"Fine, fine, no complaints. Belle here's been lifting my spirits with stories about her kids."

"Oh, you know her family as well?"

"Yeah, I have dinner at her house at least once a week. Don't I, Belle?"

Belle smiled down at him.

"Belle's a good cook."

"I'm sure, but you know there are some things you shouldn't eat, Poppa. A man your age has to worry about his arteries."

"A man my age has to get as much out of life as he can in the short time he's got left." He and Belle chuckled.

"So . . . Belle, do you work?"

"Yeah, Elaine, I do."

"At what?"

"I work at White Tower. I'm a waitress. That's where I met Phil. He one of my best customers."

"I see." Her eyes ran the length of Belle's body. "Well . . . Belle, if you wouldn't mind, I'd like to speak with Poppa alone. Family business."

"I probably been here too long anyway," Belle said as she gathered her coat and purse. "I got to get outta here in time to catch that bus. If I don't catch the next one, I'll be late for work."

With that, she kissed Phil on the forehead and nodded to Elaine. That was the last time Belle saw Phil. She came back to the hospital a couple of days later, but there was someone else in his bed. Andy said that Phil's folks put him in a nursing home out by them and that they gave the T-bird to one of his granddaughters.

Belle's Youngest

It was kind of like that movie, *The Landlord*, the one that Lou Gossett played in long before he won the Oscar or played that alien. In *The Landlord*, he played this black man who was just trying to make it. During the fifties and part of the sixties, he'd claimed his Blackfoot or some kind of American Indian heritage, trying to be anything other than a descendant of African slaves. Even though it's clear that as dark as Lou Gossett is, he can't readily pass for too much else. Now in the movie it was almost the seventies, and there was this black pride thing taking over, this reawakening, and he'd become a dashiki-wearing militant.

He and the fellas would sit on the stoop and plan movements that they never followed through on, but it gave them something to do because jobs were few and far between. Anyway, he ended up going crazy because his wife, Diana Sands, who looked really good in the movie, slept with this white man, the landlord, and got pregnant.

All this anger, hate, frustration, and just trying to make it that had been boiling up in him for decades spilled over. He went to chasing after her with an ax. It was a tight, anxious scene as she raced just ahead of him up the narrow stairs of the brownstone. He finally caught up with her in a dark corner, the ax hovering over her as she cringed in fear, sorrow, and guilt. But he can't hurt her. Instead, he just sort of implodes.

Every time I see that scene with him paralyzed against that nasty tenement wall sweating like a pig and clutching that ax, my throat gets dry and I can't swallow. Later, these two white men in white coats and white pants carry him out in a white straitjacket, strapped to a white-sheeted stretcher.

He sees his son, a boy of about eight or ten, straining to look at him in the ambulance, and he turns away because he's ashamed. Diana Sands tells the boy to go on away from there, and she's crying because she's ashamed and sorry. She tries to comfort Lou, but he stares hard at her and then shrinks away like he doesn't want her to touch him. She cries and calls his name soft-like. Those big sexy lips of hers are all twisted in agony, and he looks up, right in her eyes, and says, "My momma . . . all but one . . . had blue eyes . . . Uncle Harry had good hair . . . Christ has never known the horror of nappy hair in America."

I guess it must have felt sort of like that for Carlos when Belle took up with the German grocer on the corner and got caught. It started off real innocent. He let her have a few groceries on weekends when Carlos had gone off gambling. At first, the little white man was content to just brush up against her behind when they squeezed down the tight little aisles crowded with canned goods and boxes of detergent. Then he let her have a running tab. This little bald-headed motherfucker that never let you off if you were a penny short let Belle have a running tab. Of course, she never paid it with money. She'd go down to the store about twice a week herself, and the other times she'd just send one of her kids to pick up the milk or bread, ground beef or whatever she needed to make dinner that night or the kids' lunches in the morning.

A couple of the teenage girls in the neighborhood said that he had tried to lure them into the back room with battered boxes of candy and greasy five-dollar bills that he held out to them in his sweaty palms. Rumor was that he had a little cot in the storage room. When he took up with Belle, he hired this young black kid, a four-eyed skinny dude that read a lot, to put stock on the shelves and man the register when he was busy.

Anyway, when Belle got pregnant, it was no big thing. She and Carlos already had a house full; it was like an assembly line over there. Soon as one started toddling around on two unsteady feet, Carlos would pop another one in the oven. They were OK kids, looked mostly like Belle, and they were all dark because Belle was dark, and Carlos was one of those black Cubans with shiny, kind of curly hair. Looked like an East Indian or something. Nobody thought anything about it until Belle brought the baby home. It was so white, it was red. Eyes weren't blue, but they were this greenish color just like the grocer's on the corner.

And Belle loved that baby; she held it all the time. Used to be when she dropped one, she'd leave it with her oldest girl, Myra, to care for, then she'd be back out running the street with my momma. But with this one, she was always sitting on the front porch holding it, and making goo-goo noises and telling it how pretty it was.

The other kids started resenting all the care and affection the baby was getting. Folks said she favored the baby because it was so light, and that Belle was color struck. Myra acted like she liked the new baby for a while. When it was brand-new, she would roll it up and down the block in that little stroller with the frilly awning. Then people started asking her if it was her baby. When she'd tell them it was her sister, they'd look at her strange . . . like she had done something wrong. So, she just stopped taking it for walks, and sometimes when Belle wasn't there and Myra had to keep the baby, she'd forget to give it a bottle or change its diaper. Sometimes she would sit and listen to the baby cry while she watched *Family Feud*. The other kids followed Myra's lead and started to act like the baby didn't exist. They didn't hold its little hands up to help it walk like they'd done for each other. They didn't let it gnaw on their knuckles when it was teething, and they never kissed her fat baby belly or made blubbery noises into it to make her laugh.

The night the baby was born, Carlos came back from the hospital and sat on the cement porch railing. He nodded at Momma and Margaret, who were lounging in the two lawn chairs we kept on the porch. Then he flopped down and pulled out a cigarette, lit it, and took a long draw. Momma and Margaret had been sitting on the porch most of the evening watching the kids and waiting for news about Belle and the baby. The kids were lost in a game of blind man's bluff and were scattered along the sidewalk and beneath the big old elm that sat just at the curb. I wasn't quite sixteen yet so I couldn't date, and it was too hot in the apartment. So, I'd pulled one of our dining chairs into a far corner of the porch, tucked in my earplugs, and was bent on ignoring everyone.

After a while, Momma asked Carlos whether the baby was a boy or a girl and whether Belle had named it. He just shook his head and kept smoking Camel after Camel, thumping the still warm butts into the grass below. Then he started crying, quiet at first. But the burden was too heavy, and he broke down, burying his wet face in his hands. *"¡Cabrón!"* he cursed himself. *"¡Cabrón!"* Then he went to calling Belle every kind of bitch and saying that he wasn't going to let her put "the horns" on him, wasn't going to let her steal his manhood, that he would kill the bitch and that fucking German too.

Now of course the grocer wasn't the first man Belle had been with outside her marriage bed, but she must have been being very careful because all of her other kids matched. Either she just got caught with the grocer, or she was color struck like they said and was trying to lighten up her litter. Anyway, after about a pack of cigarettes, Carlos got up, put his hands in his pockets, and headed toward 12th Street. He didn't come back for a week, and Belle and the baby had been home a good three days.

Carlos was sober when he came back, which was a surprise. Belle was sitting on the porch, brushing the fine little hairs on the baby's head with a finger and kissing its fat red cheeks. It was a warm day, and everybody was hanging out on their front porches trying to catch a breeze. He climbed the short flight of concrete stairs and stood there for a minute looking down at them before he took a seat on the brick banister in front of Belle's chair. Aiming his body at her, he said nothing, but his face was somewhere between a scowl and bewilderment. She got up to get the bottle that she had left heating on the stove, and she held the baby out to Carlos, who didn't even pretend to raise his hands to take it. He looked at her like she was crazy for thrusting that wiggling white baby flesh in his direction.

"Bitch!" he said clearly and in an even tone. Then he stood up, and walked back down the stairs without looking back. Belle had the nerve to act surprised.

A few minutes later, police cars and later an ambulance surrounded the grocer's store. According to the four-eyed clerk, Carlos had simply gone up to the old German and asked if he knew who he was. The grocer had stammered something about, "No sir," because he could see the anguish and probably the danger in Carlos's eyes. Without any warning, the clerk said Carlos just started beating the shit out of the little man, and when he pulled out the switchblade, the clerk ran out the door and down to the barbershop, where he called the police.

The grocer lived. He must have been in the hospital for a while because his store was closed for nearly three months, and he had a limp when he came back. Carlos got shot once in the arm by the police because he wouldn't drop the knife. He was in the hospital for a while too because they beat him pretty bad. They charged him with possession of a concealed weapon, assault with intent to kill, resisting arrest, and I don't know what else. His court-appointed attorney plea-bargained, and he got off with five to ten at Jackson.

Belle never acknowledged the grocer as the baby's father. She figured she was married to Carlos so he was the baby's daddy. When her girlfriends tried to bring up the subject, they soon found out where she stood and never brought it up again, at least not in front of Belle.

The baby was a girl and Belle named her Cassandra.

The Little Apollo

By the time Cassandra graduated high school, she had grown tired of working at the Tower. The money was too slow so she got a job as a waitress at a midtown strip club. The Little Apollo was a narrow building squeezed in between a used bookstore and a veteran's counseling center. Business was good because the bartender had a reputation for pouring a solid shot and the dancers were top quality, young and fit. Most nights the place was full of Wayne State college boys and businessmen who worked at the nearby General Motors complex.

The owner was a diminutive Greek guy named Delos Pappas. The bartender, OD, and Ajax, the bouncer, called him Papa. He encouraged the girls, the dancers and the waitresses, to call him Daddy. A straight shooter, he rarely shortchanged his employees, but he was possessive about the women who worked for him, and he liked to grab a handful of ass whenever the opportunity presented itself (which was often).

For the most part, he was even tempered, but Pappas had a thing about mice. He was always laying traps and obsessively checking and rebaiting them. "Fucking rats," he'd mumble while breaking the cheese into trap-sized chunks. "Goddamn nerve, sneaking in where they're not invited," he'd curse as he tested the tiny wire springs. Not that there were that many around the place. You might see one once in a while with its little neck broken under the wire of a sprung trap or hear one scratching late at night in the storeroom.

He'd pick the dead mouse up by the tail and slip it into a plastic sandwich bag. Then he'd press his thumb and a finger along the ziplock seal, a zealot's grin tugging at his lips. With an edge of the bag pinched between two fingers and held high, he'd take it out back and drop it ceremoniously into the big dumpster like he was sending it in an elevator to hell.

OD, the bartender, had been with him nearly ten years. Although OD drank a little too much, he was a master behind the bar and had a warm, slow, knowing smile that gave his leathery caramel-colored face the look of a sage. He never stole from the till, and he didn't give Pappas competition with the women because he feared Calypso's wrath. A bite-sized Latina who was also one of the dancers, she kept a watchful eye on her man.

Ajax, the bouncer, was brawny, meanspirited, and wore a permanent leer that grew more prominent when his girl, Penelope, was on the stage. But Ajax was a hound. If it had a skirt, he wouldn't quit until he'd seen what was under it. He'd caught Cassandra's scent the day she'd come in looking for a job, and he'd been sniffing up behind her ever since. Instead of yanking his chain and setting him straight, she'd just smile and swish past him because she didn't want to hurt his feelings. Cassandra had a soft heart and was always trying to save somebody's feelings.

OD and Ajax had grown up together on the near Eastside, which over the last decade or so had become a battleground lined with crumbling houses and hungry people. Both men had narrowly escaped the current of those streets and had made a life for themselves treading water. Together they had fought off cops and kinsmen. OD had gotten Ajax this job, and they were still tight, but getting older and knowing all of each other's secrets had mellowed them. They didn't hang out or run the streets together like they used to when they were young, but whenever there was a lull, they'd sit back, have a shot, and reminisce about close calls and squandered opportunities.

Penelope, Ajax's girl, had smooth copper-burnished skin stretched over a long, lean, frame. Folks at the Apollo called her Penny. She liked to wear wigs and hairpieces that hung down her back. When she was on stage, the men would whistle encouragement through their fingers as she turned her back to them and let the long thick locks swish back and forth across her near naked behind. Penny was a looker, and she could have had anybody she wanted, but she only had eyes for Ajax.

Because she wanted to ensure that she always had a piece of him, she had a baby for him, a little boy they called Tea Leaves. When he was only a few months old, he got really sick. Penelope's mother packed him in moist tea bags, hundreds of them, to bring down the fever. Penny said she was picking little bits of leaves off him for months after that. She swears that to this day when she holds him close she can smell chamomile.

Tea Leaves stayed with Penelope's mother most of the time, but they brought him down to the club once. OD, who'd had too much to drink, got to bawling. He said that Penny, sitting there holding that baby like that, reminded him of the wife and son who had left him. He got to slobbering and went to reach for the baby, and Ajax had to stop him. Calypso, who had been sulking on the side, shoved OD's shoulder and said, "*Esa puta se fue.* Who is here for you now?" She took the blubbering OD home to sober up, and Cassandra got initiated into bartending that night.

Before long, she was helping him out on the regular and eventually just assumed the role of relief bartender when OD needed a night off. She was good at it, had a green-eyed smile that made people feel like she liked them, and most of the time she did because she liked people. And even though she was light skinned, the shade white people get after they've roasted in the sun, she never put on airs, tried to talk proper, or pursed her lips like Penelope did sometimes when she was trying to impress somebody. Cassandra was always regular, and when she was talking to someone she might touch them on an arm or a shoulder because she truly felt warm toward them.

She got good tips, and Pappas paid her a fair wage. She did alright, bought new clothes, music, and even a brand-new stereo system. Then she started wanting a car and a place of her own. It didn't take her long to realize that she couldn't manage all the things she wanted on a barmaid's salary. So, she told Pappas—Daddy to her—that she wanted to dance.

He said OK, but he wanted to send her to a school up in Toronto that trained exotic dancers. He figured if she was going to dance, she should do it right because his girls were high quality, and not only did they have to look good, they had to have style. Besides, she might pick up something new to share with the other girls, something that might spice up their acts. The prospect of going to Toronto was a boon. Cassandra had been across the river to Windsor once, on a dinner date with a boy, but Toronto was a whole new world.

She was gone three months. She had worked a couple of clubs in Toronto to try out her stuff and had considered staying, but she owed Pappas because he'd paid for the classes and had sent her money to help her with expenses until she could fund her own way.

She came back with a stock of costume stuff—spangles, feathers, body paints, glitter glue, pasties, tassels, G-strings in every color and fabric, and a collection of wigs and hairpieces. On Monday afternoons, when the Apollo was closed, she shared her stock and the new moves she learned with the other girls. They swapped costumes, practiced dance steps, hip action, pole acrobatics, and painted themselves with glitter masks and oily paint. Daddy had Chinese takeout brought in, OD lined up the shots, and the girls ate, drank, danced, and laughed a lot.

Pappas liked watching the girls and took to coming in early afternoons when the club was mostly empty and the girls practiced their acts. He would sit on the far side of the bar watching as he sipped the thick coffee that OD made just for him. When Cassandra took the stage, he moved closer. Sometimes he got excited and shouted something in Greek. Cassandra would toss him one of the seductive smiles she'd learned in Toronto, and he would turn red and take a hasty sip of his thick black coffee.

He took to bringing her flowers—a rose, a bunch of daisies wrapped in green tissue paper, and later red, red carnations when she said they were her favorite because they lived the longest. Standing half a foot over him, she'd lean down and kiss his forehead. Then she'd say, "Daddy, you're so good to me." And he would smile and stand on his tiptoes trying to reach her lips. But she would giggle and slip away.

She was happy. The dancing made her feel beautiful and free. The money was good, and Pappas didn't make her hustle drinks afterward like they did at some clubs. She bought a little used Ford Fiesta and got her own place, a tiny apartment only a couple of blocks from the club. She dated some, mostly boys she had gone to high school with, slept with one occasionally just to keep in practice, but there was no one important, no one she wanted to share her real life with.

Then Pappas hired Minerva, a tall white girl with dark hair and slate-colored eyes. When she stepped out onto the stage, she wore a long metallic tunic with slits that allowed glimpses of long swatches of smooth, tight thighs and the sides of plump breasts when she moved. Silver sandals with straps that laced up her calves completed the costume, and she carried a silver thonged whip. She danced to Wagner, operatic music, and her aggressive moves left her drenched in sweat as a blue gel bathed the stage during the finale. When she shed the tunic, the light made her nipples and the tiny triangle between her legs glow. When the light began to flick on and off, her skin began to shimmer, and as she writhed and squirmed, her sex seemed to pulse and throb to the cackle of the thunder that rose in the background.

Minerva took to Cassandra right away. She was always brushing Cassandra's hair or plying her with new eye shadows or colognes. She told her about other cities and the clubs she had worked. Cassandra talked to her about growing up in Detroit. They talked about men, and Cassandra confided that she'd never been in love and talked about how annoying it was when guys gave her a hard time, calling her a snooty bitch, when she told them she wasn't interested. She told her about the time Ajax cornered her in the alley just outside the club. How he'd pressed her into the bricks and grabbed her between her legs, saying that just thinking about her cream made his dick hard. And she confessed that the only reason Ajax was halfway leaving her alone was because he didn't want to cross the boss.

They started scheduling days off together so they could go shopping or see a movie. Sometimes they'd sleep nights at each other's apartment. Cassandra would take long hot baths while Minerva popped popcorn and made Kool-Aid. Then Minerva would have her shower while Cassandra spread the picnic pallet out in the living room in front of the TV.

One night, while they lay on the pallet, Minerva tucked a fallen curl behind Cassandra's ear. Then Minerva was kissing her, and Cassandra let her, so Minerva bent her head to suck at Cassandra's nipples through the thin nightgown as she trailed her long fingers down the center of her back. Cassandra really didn't know what to say because she liked Minerva and didn't want to hurt her. She was always trying to save somebody's feelings. She lay there stiff-like and just let her, but it started to feel warm and tingly, and she did like Minerva. So she reached down and touched Minerva's hair, and then they were kissing again, and it felt good.

It began like that, and it was good because Minerva was easy to get along with, and she was quiet about her love. She didn't kiss in public or do anything to let the people at the Little Apollo know that they were together.

Cassandra was happy. She liked dancing; it made her feel beautiful and free. The money was good, and she had someone to love her, someone who knew all about her and accepted her the way she was.

One night after finishing her number, Cassandra left the stage and made her way through the narrow hallway that led back to the dressing room. She was breathing hard and was all sweaty from the lights and the dancing. Minerva, just about to go on, was all fresh and cool as she stood in the dark just beyond the stage.

"Baby," Minerva whispered, putting her cool arms around Cassandra's dripping midriff. "You looked so good out there, you made me wet." She moved Cassandra toward the wall, pressing her cool body against Cassandra's sweaty one, and ran her tongue along the seam of Cassandra's lips. Minerva's tongue was darting in and out of Cassandra's half-opened mouth as thunder and lightning rose behind them, announcing Minerva's entrance. She pressed a quick kiss to Cassandra's lips, one last peck, and made her way onto the stage.

Cassandra leaned against the wall trembling, aching at the absence. Then, remembering where she was, she looked around, and at the far end of the hallway she could see Pappas's pale face peering through the darkness. Embarrassed, she straightened up and made her way toward the dressing room. As she got closer, she could see that he held a red carnation, and when she got near him, he refused to let her pass. He was short, but he was wide. She tried a smile on and allowed the tips of her breasts to brush against his chest as she moved aside, her eyes shining playfully, but it only seemed to aggravate him. He responded by pushing her against the wall and holding her there. Angrily, she pushed back.

A funny smirk played on his lips, and he cupped her naked breast and said, "You owe me."

"I don't owe you a damn thing," she said as she peeled his hand off.

He looked at her a long time, and she tried to cast him a look of defiance. Then he threw the carnation in her face and said, "Have it your way then," and he turned and walked away.

After that, Pappas started complaining about everything. He'd start in early, his quick little steps echoing as he made his way across the room, peering into every crevice from one end of the bar to the other. A storm gathered in his face as he raged about how the girls took too long on their breaks, customers weren't drinking enough, and stock was always low. When he said the last thing, he'd lean toward the bar and eye OD.

OD ignored him and continued shining up the glasses with the dry towel and holding them up to the light to check for water spots.

After a few minutes of uncomfortable silence, Pappas would start ranting about how mice were ruining his storeroom, his arms flailing in the air, and then he'd start in on the girls again. He didn't know if he could keep all them all on . . . "and since Minerva was the last hired, fair is fair."

But Pappas continued to seethe and ply his poison.

"That Minerva is a very large woman," he said to Ajax, who lounged on a stool at the bar. "There's something *funny* about her."

"Yeah, she a big bitch," Ajax agreed.

Pappas looked at his feet and then up at Ajax. "Look how she carries herself. And I've never seen her with a man."

Ajax nodded. "You know, you're right. Neither have I."

OD just listened and continued shining glasses with a dry towel and holding them up to the light to check for water spots.

Eventually Pappas caught Ajax by himself. "Have you noticed that Cassandra has been spending a lot of time with Minerva?" he asked.

"You think the two of them . . . ?" Ajax drew back, a look of disgust on his face.

"It would be such a waste if that was the case," Pappas said as he shook his head sadly and then added, "A relationship like that could really ruin a girl like Cassandra."

Ajax looked thoughtful, like he was trying to figure out where Pappas was going with all this talk.

"You know what they say about those kind of women. That they can spoil a good woman, make her lose her taste for men," he added in a confidential tone.

Ajax shook his head and laughed. "Papa, you something, always hanging on to them tales. Ain't nothing a good man cain't cure. Ain't no woman immune to a good hard piece of meat."

"You don't seem to be having much luck with Cassandra," Pappas said, laughing with Ajax.

"Papa, you always underestimate me. How much you wanna bet that I cain't get a piece of that ass?" Ajax cupped himself and chuckled just loud enough for Pappas to hear.

A few days later as the girls got ready for the first show, Pappas was still pressing. "A friend of mine who owns a club in Warren said his business doubled when the girls started drinking with the customers," he said. "Guys always buy the best when they're treating a pretty girl." He grinned as he hoisted a tiny black-leather-clad foot onto a wooden chair near the door of the dressing room. Penelope nodded, surprised he hadn't asked it of them sooner. And Pappas, as though he'd received a burst of encouragement, continued, "You know how a man likes to show off for a beautiful woman."

It was a hot day, but inside the club it was a little cooler because the overhead lights were muted and the air conditioner was trying to work. The only lights on were the small ones over the bar and a couple at the base of the stage. Pappas stood in front of the stage, the footlights providing an eerie reddish backlighting. Penelope and Calypso were sitting at the table nearest the stage nursing lukewarm coffee. A couple of the barmaids sat at a table behind them. Cassandra was leaning up against the bar, waiting for OD to finish stirring the ice cubes into a tall glass of pineapple juice. He swiped the bottom of the glass with a damp towel and placed the paper coaster and the chilled glass in front of her.

Pappas was going on about how long he'd been in the business, how if he didn't make any money "nobody sitting here would," and how he didn't feel like folks were pulling together like they should. "There'll have to be some changes," he barked. "You're going to have to get your asses in gear, if you want to keep your jobs." OD was grinning and wiping down the bar. He caught Cassandra's eye, tilted his head toward Pappas, and shook it. She shrugged and sipped pineapple juice. "Trying to keep his empire intact," she whispered. "Little bitty motherfucker, think he Napoleon." OD's grin got bigger.

"First," Pappas said, holding up a pudgy finger, "the girls are going to have to come out and have a drink or two with the customers after they finish their number. These college boys don't seem to want to buy nothing but beer. They need a little encouragement so they'll buy hard liquor and mixed drinks."

Then he went on about how business had been falling off and that's why he had to let Minerva go, and how all this "show-boat shit had to go. This ain't no Ziegfeld Follies. The guys come here to see tits and ass, not some modern dance bullshit. Shake your ass, show your tits, then go dry off, put on something skimpy, and get back out on the floor."

That's when Ajax came up behind Cassandra and started rubbing himself up against her ass and telling her how he didn't see why she "could be into women cause I know ain't no woman got what I got."

She looked at him out of the side of her eye like he was a piece of horse shit, and then she moved farther down the bar, away from him. But he followed her, slipped his arm around her waist, pulled the hem of her brand-new silk blouse out of her jeans, and ran his hands over the bare skin of her back. Before he could say the soft words that were perched on his tongue, she turned and slapped the shit out of him.

He grabbed at her, ripping her blouse as she pulled away. Just then, Penelope fell between them and screamed at Ajax to stop. He pushed Penelope to the side and said, "Bitch, you bet-ta get outta my way." But by then, OD had come out from behind the bar and was holding on to Ajax saying, "How you gon act man with yo woman sitting right there?" Then he was talking low to Ajax and backing him away. But Ajax kept shout-ing things like, "That dykie bitch got her fucking nerve," and "Don't no ho' put they hands in my face!"

Cassandra pulled her ripped blouse around her and went over to help Penelope, who was sprawled on the floor, but Penelope pushed her hand away and shot her an evil look that said, "Don't touch me." Then she reached past Cassandra to Calypso, who was also bending down to help her. Cassandra moved out of the way, and Penelope and Calypso went off to the ladies room together.

Pappas went behind the bar and poured himself a cup of that thick black coffee and acted as though nothing had happened.

Two weeks after the meeting and Pappas was still nagging the girls about not working hard enough, especially Cassandra. He said she wasn't friendly enough, she took too long to get out front after her number, and she never stayed long enough to do any good. Once he even had her come in early so he could talk to her alone about how she could "improve her work habits." As he listed his concerns, he poured a thin line of a white powdery poison along the edge of the floor just where the baseboards met the floor planks. She listened to what he had to say, then explained that she liked to take a shower after a show, but he just said that sometimes a little sweat turned men on and that she was just too particular about some things. He didn't even look at her as he spoke. All of his attention was centered on the box of rat poison. Every time he came to a place where there was a crack or crevice in the wall or the floor, he'd pour out an extra bit of poison and then whisk it in with the small blush brush he kept in his pocket. When she realized the conversation was at an end, she just shrugged and headed back to the dressing room to prep for the first show.

Ajax hadn't said anything to Penelope since the meeting where she'd jumped between him and Cassandra. He just glared at her whenever she entered the room.

Penelope had come to work early. She wanted to talk to Ajax, and he had been dodging her. She figured she might catch him when he was in a good mood if she came around when he was helping OD open up the club. In the past, she noticed that when it was just him and OD, Ajax seemed more easygoing.

Penelope had on an airy summer dresses. Her hair was swept up off her neck into a barrette that had two cloth daisies on it. She beamed at Ajax from across the room because she had checked her reflection several times in the mirror before she left the house, and she knew she looked good. Plus, she had seen Ajax's broad smile as he and OD laughed and talked as they took the chairs down off the tables. Standing across the room near the entrance, she summoned some courage. "Ajax, can I talk to you a minute?" Her voice was shaky, almost a whisper.

When he turned to her, his smile vanished, and he got a funny look on his face, like he was doing or thinking something he didn't want her to know about. But he said, "Sure baby. Take a seat. Give me a minute." He put a few more chairs down and lit a cigarette before making his way to the table where she'd chosen to sit.

"What you doing here so early?" he asked as he dusted the cigarette ash he'd meant to flick on the floor from his shoe. He stood looking down on her, one foot resting on a rung of a chair.

"I been missing you," she began. "Where you been, Ajax? Only time I see you is when we here. You don't never come see Tea Leaves, and we ain't spent no *quality* time with each other in over a month."

"I been busy, baby. You know I got to take care a my other hustle. I'm a working man. I ain't got no time to sit up and play house with you."

"When you start feeling that way, Ajax? You used to . . ."

"Things change, baby."

Penelope studied her fingernails for a while, then she looked up at him, not directly into his face, but sort of at his nose.

"Well, Ajax, I just wanted to tell you that I'm gonna have another baby, and I was hoping that you . . . I don't know . . . might be glad about it."

At that, his jaw dropped, and he kicked the chair that he had been resting his foot on. It fell backward and made a loud clattering sound.

"What the fuck you think I am, you dumb bitch? Don't you know how to take care of yourself?"

Suddenly, he straightened and extracted a wad of bills from his pants pocket. He took a step away from the table, unwound four fifties, and flung them across the table. Then, leaning toward her and lowering his voice an octave, he snarled, "Take that and go get yourself fixed. I don't want no mo goddamn babies. What the fuck you think you trying to do to me?"

Penelope just started crying and looking at him like she didn't believe what he was saying. Or that he would talk to her like that in front of OD, who was standing behind the bar wiping glasses and acting like he hadn't heard a thing. While they sat, others had come in. Pappas stood in the doorway of his office, holding a box of poison as he looked around the room to see what the commotion was. And Cassandra, who Penelope wanted to slap because she had the nerve to look like she felt sorry for somebody, was standing just inside the front door like she'd just witnessed the worst of it.

Ajax turned back to Penny, a sad look on his face like he could feel her pain, but he didn't want to undo the breakup. So he sat down and tried to let her know what he was feeling, or at least what he felt like they had to do without hurting her too much.

"We just don't need another baby right now," he said in a softer voice. "I care about you, baby, but I cain't handle it. I got too much going on right now."

He figured Penny had had a baby for him, and she said she was carrying another one, so she had to love him. And he could get her back whenever he wanted, when he had time.

But right now, he just wanted a little air. And he was glad that Cassandra and Pappas had seen that he had cut Penny loose, and that he was free. Anyhow, he just wanted Penny to back off for a while. He figured he could use this baby thing like a crowbar and create a gap to pry Penny lose. Then when he was ready he could use that same crowbar to hammer everything back into place and close the hole, if he wanted her back then. Ajax started talking quickly and very softly, his words rushing and faltering, rushing and faltering.

"Look, baby, I don't mean to be hurting you . . . It's just that . . . you making me feel all closed in . . . like a goddamn fly in a jar that somebody forgot to put the holes in . . . Baby, I just need some time."

She looked at his face, which had softened considerably because it no longer held the anger, but there was still something hard and cold about the way he held his mouth, the way his eyes looked her over. So she decided it was useless to say anything else. Besides, she figured she knew Ajax. When he calmed down and thought it out, he'd be back knocking on her door talking about how he didn't mean it. So Penny grabbed the bills off the table— she could always use the money. She stuffed them into her purse and left the bar without saying anything else to anyone.

Meanwhile, Minerva tried to convince Cassandra to move to Toronto with her. But Cassandra kept saying that she just needed a little time to think, to clear the smoke out of her head. Having waited as long as her funds allowed, Minerva sold her meager furnishings, threw the rest of her belongings into a suitcase, and bought a one-way train ticket to Toronto. Pappas continued to rant and harass the girls, especially Cassandra, about not putting enough life into the dancing, about declining profits, too much overhead, and the mice that he swore were overrunning the place.

As Minerva boarded the tunnel bus that would take her to the train station, she told Cassandra to "tell that Ajax if he bothers you again, I'm going to come back and fuck him up." They hugged and cried and kissed each other good-bye. Minerva promised, "I'll be waiting for you." Cassandra cried some more, and then she drove her little Ford Fiesta on back to the Little Apollo.

That night was a particularly hot one. The air conditioner had been shorting out all week, so Calypso had brought a fan in from home for the dressing room. The girls kept sneaking away from the floor to sit under the fan and sip ice water, but Pappas had come banging on the door more than once to chase the girls back out.

Cassandra had just finished her number and was breaking for the fan in the dressing room when she passed Pappas in the hall.

"Fifteen-minute break, then out on the floor," he barked at her back as she pushed through the dressing room door.

"Asshole," she breathed as she plopped down into the chair that was positioned directly in the fan's path.

She closed her eyes and threw back her head, enjoying the gusts of air that caused the sweat running down the crevice between her breasts to chill. She jumped and nearly fell from the chair when a finger ran the length of her neck and halfway down her back as though it was chasing the droplets of sweat. Ajax leaned over her. "I been waiting for you."

The chair fell over as she jumped up and backed away. "Get out of here, Ajax."

He liked the way she looked, all damp and sweaty, and he could just imagine how wet she'd be. Penelope said that in order to turn on an audience, you had to feel turned on. The money and winning the bet would be the icing; Cassandra was the pound cake, rich and moist. He had waited so long. Just like Penny and all the others, when he gave it to her, she would melt, moan, and beg for more. He knew bitches.

He used his sexy voice. "But baby, I been waiting to get you alone like this for a long time. I figure you just be acting stuck-up cause we be in front of other people. Besides, it's like OD say: you and Penelope is kinda like friends, and you don't want her to know. But she don't have to know. I know you like me. I see how you look at me. Come here."

He reached for her, and she slapped his hand and slipped past him to the other side of the room near the dressing table. Powder and bottles fell to the floor as she pushed them aside looking for a weapon, but before she could find one Ajax had tackled her, and they wrestled, falling to the floor. They fought hard. Cassandra's knees and fists made sharp thrusts into Ajax's body, but before long he had her pinned down.

"You stupid motherfucker, can't you see when you not wanted?" she screamed between breaths as she ripped long, jagged strips of skin from his face with her nails. He held her down, his forearm on her neck, and he touched his face and came away with blood on his hand. "Bitch!" he hollered as his hardened fists struck her cheek twice, maybe three times. The first time her head jerked sideways, and her mouth opened; after the second or third, she stopped struggling. He hadn't meant to get so rough with her, but it wasn't like she didn't have it coming. Some women played hard to get, pushed a man to his limit because they liked it rough. He didn't mind playing that game.

The tussling had him pumped up, and he was tearing at her kimono when he smelled the smoke and heard the commotion in the hall outside the dressing room door. He pulled himself up to his knees as he strained to hear what was going on beyond the closed door. He had waited a long time for this half-white piece of tail, but it wasn't worth dying for, and the confusion in the hall sounded serious. He stood, straightened his clothes, and with the tip of his shoe, he nudged Cassandra's leg. Her head was turned to the side, and he thought she might be crying. Women like to put on a show, but he didn't have time for all that.

"Come on, girl, get up," he urged. "We need to get out of here."

The commotion outside got louder, and she still wasn't moving so he bent over her to see why. When he saw that she was out cold, he pulled what was left of the cotton kimono around her and sat her up in a chair. Her chin dropped to her chest, but she didn't fall so he left her there and headed toward the door. The room was getting cloudy with smoke, and the smell of burning wood and plastic. A part of him worried that he'd really hurt her, but the larger part of him wanted out of this room. He'd figure out what to do about her when he found out what was going on outside.

Patting down his Afro with one hand, he twisted the knob with the other. The door didn't open. Then he began to pull at the knob and beat on the door. "Who locked this goddamn door from the outside?" he screamed. But the door would not budge. Frightened, he began to kick and ram the door with his shoulder. He shouted for OD, Pappas, and then for Penelope. The smoke clogged his throat, and he couldn't breathe. He grabbed some flimsy cloth that one of the girls had left on that makeup table and covered his mouth. It didn't help much, and after a while he was huddled on the floor gasping for air.

A crowd gathered in the street; police in short-sleeved summer uniforms pressed them back as the firemen retrieved their hose. An emergency medical crew climbed out of the charred bar's front entrance carrying the first stretcher. Cassandra's barely clothed body lay limply on the crisp white sheets, her lemon skin blackened by the heavy smoke. The crew slid the stretcher into the ambulance, covered the body, and sped, siren blaring, to the nearest emergency room. The second crew came out of the smoldering building bent under the bulk of Ajax's body as it sprawled on the stretcher. They followed the same procedure, hindered only by the screams and frail limbs of Penelope, who threw herself across Ajax's body. OD plucked her hands from the corpse, carried her a distance away, and held her firmly even as her body melted in his arms.

The fire marshal said it was an electrical fire common to these older buildings. Pappas collected the insurance and built a fancy new place on Eight Mile near Southfield. He called it the Coliseum. In a month the Little Apollo had been torn down, the rubble shoveled onto trucks and carted away. A couple of weeks later, patches of green and brownish weeds shot up, their roots burrowing deep into the soil, and field mice romped and ran freely.

Margaret's Prince

It's about three in the morning and I cain't sleep, so I get up and sit on the couch. I try to get comfortable, put my feet up and scoot to the center. I rest my arm on the back of the couch so I can see out the big front window. Every once in a while a car turn down our block and speed up toward 12th Street. I tug at the shade to get a better look at the street, and it shoot up to the top of the window flapping and fluttering. I stand up on the couch real quick trying to catch it before the noise wake up the kids.

After I fix it, I pull my knees up to my chest and settle down in the far corner of the couch. The street is dark and deserted, and I can hear birds chirping. The headlights of a car light up the street for a minute, and then they gone. The car must a scared the birds cause they quiet now.

That old man that live cross the street is staggering down the sidewalk, on his way home from the after-hour joint round the corner. He stop to straighten hisself before he climb the stairs and disappear into the doorway.

After a while, Lorraine—that's the girl that live in the house kitty-corner to ours—come out a her door. She turn to check the door a second time to make sure it's locked. Then she drop her house key in her purse and head down the stairs to her car. It's a old Ford, but it's running, and she the only woman on the block that got her own car. A few of the other women can drive, and they boyfriends or husbands let them use they car sometimes. But that ain't like having your own and being able to get up and go whenever you want to. Lorraine got a good job at the post office. She work funny hours, but she ain't got no man so she don't have to answer to nobody.

Don't nobody come down the block or out they door for a long time. Out there in them trees, the sparrows singing some kinda lonely blues song. So, I get my latest copy of *True Confession* and try to tune 'em out. I'm trying to read this story about this girl in love with her stepbrother, but I ain't getting very far. My mind keep drifting, and my eyes keep wandering back to that ole empty street.

I hear my baby, Belinda, in the hallway. She calling me. I hear her soft tiny voice go, "Momma." She being quiet so she won't wake up her sister, and she scared to come out here. I don't say nothing so she call me again, "Momma." Then she come stand in the doorway of the living room, pulling at them fat pigtails and rubbing her eyes, her round belly poking out her cotton nightie. She quiet for a while, waiting for me to send her back to bed or fuss about her being up, but she so cute I just smile. Then she say, "Momma, I cain't sleep." I hold out my arms to her, and she come tumbling in. I squeeze her tight, and we sit there all snuggled up for a while. I can feel her warm little body as I kiss her head and rock her.

I say let's go get a glass a warm milk, and she ask can she have some chocolate in it. I tell her OK, and she beat me to the kitchen. We cut on lights, and Belinda start pulling things outta the cabinets like its daytime. She looking for the saucepan in the bottom cupboards, rattling pans, pulling 'em all out, and stacking 'em up. I shoosh her, and tell her to hurry up and bring me that saucepan. She trots it over and then start putting the pans back in the cupboard extra slow and careful so as not to make no noise. That Belinda always make me smile.

I'm stirring the milk and Belinda standing on a chair watching and telling me about something that happen to her at school today, but my mind keep going back to Richard out on that road. He shoulda been in a hour ago. I'd been laying in bed wide-awake for the last three or four hours, tossing and turning, listening for the rig to pull up. I'd give a start every time I heard a car pass. Then when it'd come to me that it was just a car, I'd get this slow, sinking feeling. So I tried to stop listening, tried to go to sleep, but my eyes would keep popping open, and my ears would follow every voice automatic-like. That's why I just decided to go on an get up and wait for him.

I hate myself for being like this. I remember when Nick and me was staying together. He wasn't no good, but I dug me some Nick. He worked the foundry and used to always say, "When you work hard, you deserve to play hard, and I damn show works hard." When me and him first got together, he was all over me all the time. I couldn't breathe. But I guess he got used to me, and he start coming home later and later.

At first, I used to worry whether something had happened to him. Then I start worrying that he had another woman. We went through a time when I argued and cried about it every waking minute, with him telling me that I was just too jealous, that I didn't want him to have no fun. Then I just got used to it. He'd come slipping in three, four, five in the morning, and then he crawl in bed with his back to me. I'd glance at the clock then go on back to sleep.

I argued at him from time to time, but it was just words to let out my frustration. What really tore it was when I went to Benton Harbor to visit my Momma. I came back early cause I can only take Momma so long. Anyway, that dog wouldn't let me in my own house. Come holding the door talking about, "Wait a minute, baby." Talking about he taking care a something he don't want the kids to see. Telling me to come back in a half hour. I knew he had some woman up in my house.

I wanted to die, but first I wanted to cut his lying, cheating heart out. The kids was standing next to me in that hallway looking real curious so I had to be cool, but I couldn't stop the tears.

I took the kids over to my sister's house, and when I came back he was gone. So, I took all of his stuff: his component set, the records that he had been collecting for the last twenty years; all his clothes, underwear, suits, hats, shoes; an even the cup, knife, and can of Magic Shave he had up in the bathroom cabinet. I took it all and threw it off the top porch into the front yard. Then I gave the old man that live on the corner five dollars to change my locks.

After Nick, I was through with men, period. I went to work and raised my kids. Central High School had the cleanest bathrooms in the city. Belle say I was putting all my pent-up sex drive into my job. But I didn't care. I had my job and my kids, and I didn't need no dirty, lying, cheating dog of a man.

Then one night Belle dragged me out with her, and I met Richard, the sweetest man in the whole world. He treat my girls like they his own. Give 'em allowance every Friday, and he take us to movies and once to Edgewater Park. He do more for them than they daddies. See, Belinda is Nick's. I had Barbara, my oldest—she eight—by my first husband.

Richard treat me as if I'm the prettiest, smartest lady in the world. It's funny cause when I first saw him, I said to myself I'll let this big old dude buy me some drinks. When he told me about owning his own truck, I say, well, maybe I might go out with him. But he just grow on you. He such a good man . . . and I don't want him to turn out to be like Nick.

I pour Belinda and me a cup a cocoa, and we turn on the late, late movie. I turn the sound down real low cause I don't want to wake up Barbara. Belinda chattering on and on about school. It's all new to her cause she just started in September. She leaning up against me, sipping her hot chocolate. I know she gon tease Barbara tomorrow about how she got to stay up late an have cocoa.

The movie on the late, late show is *All the Fine Young Cannibals*. I've seen it three or four times before, but I'm glad it's on cause it's a good one. Robert Wagner play this poor musician who knocked Natalie Wood up. But in the end, after all the troubles, Natalie Wood end up with this really good man who forgives her past mistakes and accepts her baby as his own. I cry every time I see it.

Pearl Bailey in it too. She a blues singer who love this man really bad, but he don't love her. She singing now, and it's a sad song like she hurt so bad she about to die. She singing how she give him everything, but he still leave her. The trumpet cries with her, and I wonder where Richard is. Belinda try to sip her hot chocolate slow, but pretty soon she finish. She look up at me and ask, "Do I gotta go to bed now?"

I smile an say, "Naw, you can stay up a little while longer," cause it feel good having her warm body next to me.

She sleeping now, her head in my lap. I smooth down the damp ends of hair and touch her soft, soft face. The radiator is hissing and sputtering.

Pearl Bailey done died, and they got this New Orleans–style funeral, but it's in a juke joint and everybody crying. I look out the window at the streetlight on the corner. Everything else is dark. It's a sad funeral so I cry and hope Richard don't turn out to be another Nick.

Robert Wagner's new woman try to commit suicide cause she cain't get him to love her cause he still in love with Natalie Wood. He treat the girl real cold too. He don't care what she do or how much she show her love, and she just get more and more pitiful. I cry for her too cause I know how it is to try to make something work, and you just cain't figure out the right thing to do.

Maybe there was some kind of accident. Sometimes truck drivers fall asleep at the wheel. Maybe he in the hospital. Maybe I should call the hospital or the police.

If he was gon be late, he shoulda called. I stroke Belinda's back and lift the material of her gown away from her skin cause she sweating. Then I take the bottom of my pajama top and wipe around the edges of her hair.

Natalie Wood done left her ole man cause she feeling guilty about lying and cheating. Now she sorry cause she realize she love him. I heard that one before. Guess men be getting burnt too. I smile and wait for the good part when he come get her.

He standing on the old rickety back porch playing with the baby now. She come to the screen door cause she hear the baby making noises. She been washing dishes so she wipe her hands on her apron and peek through the screen. It's one of them old wood houses, propped up on bricks, like they got down south. He look at her with this sad longing in his eyes and say, "I want you back, Salome." I cry happy tears as the credits roll over they faces.

I'm smiling an thinking how much I love this movie when I hear Richard's rig pull up in the vacant lot next door. I lean over the back of the couch so I can see his truck better. He rummage around inside the cab a minute. Then he turn on the inside light and look at hisself in the rearview mirror. When he check his teeth, I cain't help but smile. He pull out his pick and jab it into his Afro a couple of times before he climb down from the cab. He look real tired, but he look good to me. That Richard is really something. I'm humming that Billie Holiday song about the man I love as I scoop Belinda up and head back to the bedrooms.

Westside

The Siege

It was early June, the best time of the year. Clear blue skies with sketchy bits of white clouds; the temperature was around seventy-five, a typical summer day in Detroit. Women in jeans or cotton housedresses and a few nuns in the new just-below-the-knee habits fussed round the long, narrow tables that lined both sides of Belmont Street from John R to Woodward. They draped white tablecloths or old sheets over the rough wooden tabletops and arranged paperback books, old *Jet* and *Ebony* magazines, comic books, used tools, costume jewelry, tarnished chains, and hoop earrings, lining them up in neat rows. Others had faded jeans, baby clothes, mismatched silverware, dishes, and knickknacks stacked in neat piles and groupings. The Cathedral of the Most Blessed Sacrament was hosting its Annual Community Flea Market.

Stretching along the left side of the street and serving as the market's backdrop was the massive brick church with its attached rectory that housed nuns and visiting priests, and the church's community center, where the neighborhood kids played ball and practiced doo-wop. On the other side of the street, behind the tables, was a series of wide porches, sturdy brick and shingle homes that had been built at the turn of the century when the City began expanding to the North End.

Momma's younger sister, Jamie, had rented two tables. She had a dozen kids, who took turns swarming around her and the tables and bumping into things until she shooed them off. She'd enlisted her oldest girls, Ella and Jackie, to help her out, but they kept disappearing into the community center, where a group of boys was playing basketball.

Aunt Jamie was a housewife, but she ran numbers sometimes and knew what it meant to hustle. For years she'd had to keep the house up and feed and clothe her family on what her husband brought home from his job on the line after he'd siphoned off his liquor money. That morning she'd had a steady tide of customers, and the little money tin she kept under the table was quickly filling up. She'd even given her son, Leon, who was nearly twelve, money to buy ice cream for the younger kids. Smiling, she watched as he chased the singing ice cream truck down the street, the five-dollar bill wadded in his hand.

She turned her smile on the two young men who stood in front of her table. They weren't from the neighborhood; at least she didn't recognize either of them. But they were young, the bigger one looked older, maybe twenty. The other was maybe a couple of years younger. They looked like brothers. The older one was picking through the baby clothes, or at least he lifted the first couple of pieces in the stack of folded sleepers, and seemed to be interested. The other one was stirring a couple of necklaces, a gold-colored chain and a piece made of cowrie shells, with his finger.

To the skinny one with his finger in the jewelry, she said, "Two for a dollar." He looked at her, his eyes slightly hooded, but didn't say anything. Then he looked at his brother and grinned before looking over his shoulder, first to the right and then to the left. When he stayed quiet, she gave her attention to the other one.

"Those are in good condition, freshly washed. I even pressed them with a warm iron," Aunt Jamie said to the big guy who was looking at the onesies. "I can give you a good deal on them. Babies tend to go through two or three in a day. So, it's always good to have a few clean ones on hand."

He looked at her like she was a roach and then lifted his shirt to show her the gun he had tucked in the waist of his pants. "Give me all of your money or die, bitch," he said.

She was stunned, but Jamie had always been one to think on her feet. "Are you for real?" she asked, pretending not to believe him. "How much money you think somebody gon make out here?"

"Don't play with me, bitch," he said the words softly, but the threat was clear.

So, Jamie reached into the pocket of her skirt and pulled out the money she had been using for change, seven singles, a half roll of nickels, and a handful of dimes, quarters, and pennies she had tied loosely in an old handkerchief.

"Here," she said, holding the money out to him. She wanted to throw it at him, but he did have a gun, and she didn't want him to get mad. Her hands were sweating, and when he didn't take the money, she set it down hard on the table in front of him. She was pissed. She'd been standing out under the sun all morning, and this young blood was trying to take her hard-earned money.

"I want that money box you got under the table," the big guy said.

"What money box?" she asked.

"Don't play with me, bitch," he said.

Aunt Jamie hesitated for a minute, but her good sense got the best of her. She bent down, reached under the flap of table-cloth, and pulled the tin from its hiding place. Still, she clutched the small metal box to her chest for a few seconds before handing it over to the thief.

"Tell her to dig down in them titties and give up them bills," the younger one said. He was grinning. "That's where she keep the big money."

"Dig down in them titties and gimme them bills," the older one said. "I want all of it."

Aunt Jamie sucked her teeth, trying to think what else she could do. Then she saw her brother Ronald coming up behind the big guy. He held a small gun low in his right hand. Aunt Jamie held her breath as she watched Ronald come closer.

"Motherfuckah you must have a death wish," Uncle Ronald said as he stepped so close to the big guy he seemed to be fused into the thief's left side. Then he eyed the skinny one, who stood a couple of feet over to the right of the big guy.

Aunt Jamie took a breath. The skinny kid's eyes got big, and he took a step back and asked, "Who's this mother?"

"You fucking with my sister?" Ronald said as he pressed his own gun into the bigger guy's side. "Give the money tin back to her."

Aunt Jamie said that's when it got real crazy. The oldest would-be thief dropped the money tin on the table, whipped his gun out of his waistband, and tried to turn and aim it at Ronald, but he was too slow because Ronald never hesitates. Two shots, loud enough to make somebody go deaf, burst out. The big guy dropped his gun, clutched his side, and fell to the ground. The skinny one was all wild eyes and jitters, but he stayed put. He just stood there watching as Ronald kicked the fallen guy's gun out of reach. The little black snub-nosed piece skittered across the pavement like a scared mouse. All the while, the skinny bandit was looking down at his brother, watching him bleed all over the sidewalk like he was wondering how this could have happened.

Then Ronald, just as cool as you please, tucked his own gun into the back of his pants and pulled his shirt over it. Showing no concern for the bleeding man, he stepped around him so that he could pull his sister into his arms. "It's OK," he said to Aunt Jamie as he held her, his hand making soothing circles in the center of her back. She nodded and hugged him back, tight, relieved at having been saved.

Seconds passed, a crowd gathered, and the high-pitched sound of a siren filled the air. Aunt Jamie said that must have been when the skinny thief picked up his brother's gun and hid it. He must have thrown it into the bushes because when the cops showed up they couldn't find it. The only gun on the scene belonged to Ronald.

The place was a mass of sirens and blinking lights as an ambulance and two police cars pulled up. The police spoke to Aunt Jamie first, and then they questioned the wounded man's accomplice, who kept pointing at Ronald and frowning. When they were finished with him, they pulled Uncle Ronald off to the side and began questioning him. The skinny guy took that opportunity to step up right next to Jamie and hiss in her ear, "This ain't over, bitch." Then he darted over to where the bleeding man was being hoisted onto a stretcher. While paramedics tended to the fallen man, a couple of uniformed police interviewed the bystanders. Before the ambulance drove off, the police relieved Ronald of his gun, cuffed him, and shoved him into the back of the squad car.

Ronald was a wild card, the younger brother nobody would expect to come in and save the day. He was just as likely to start a fight at a family reunion as he was to yank the microphone from whoever was speaking and drunkenly slobber all over it about how blessed he was to be in a room with so much love.

You never knew what to expect from him. He liked the rough and tumble of street life and had been arrested a few times on minor drug charges, but nothing had ever stuck. Meanwhile, he'd earned a degree from Wayne State in fine art, and he painted large oil-on-canvas portraits, starkly vivid images of the men and women he knew from the streets. He was usually living with some loud, equally wild woman he'd picked up in a bar. Together they ran with the rhythms of the street doing or dealing drugs. He liked living the fast life, and he'd been lucky dancing the limbo just low enough to slip under and escape the police baton.

Jamie couldn't do anything but watch as the police stuffed her handcuffed brother into the squad car. But ever Ronald, he grinned over at her just before he slid into the back seat. She shook her head and smiled back at him. His grin reminded her of the black-and-white photo she'd taken of him standing in front of the tall wooden wall that separated the house they grew up in from the railroad tracks. He must have been all of nine years old, a spindly little black boy with rusty arms and legs wearing a striped T-shirt, baggy shorts, a broad grin, and that bad-boy glint in his eyes. He had that same glint in his eye just before they slammed the door of the police car.

The flea market was forced to close after that, the priest and the nuns expressing concern for everyone's safety as they talked quietly with individual parishioners and helped others pack up. Well before the sun went down, the people and tables had been cleared away, and Jamie, who lived up the block, was seated on her front porch watching the smallest of her children play blind man's bluff. That's when the car full of angry-looking *boys* pulled up in front of her house.

Jamie said that they looked to be in their late teens or early twenties. The older Plymouth sedan was going east on Belmont so it was on the other side of the street, but she could clearly see the five men, two in the front and three in the back. The one in the front on the passenger side was the skinny guy from the stickup.

The car idled in the middle of the street for a minute, maybe two, before it slowly pulled away. Jamie called the kids in and sent them upstairs to play while she hid behind the front room curtain, peeking out to see if they came back. They did, once more, driving slow and sneering up at the house. She called the police, but they told her they couldn't do anything about some-body riding past and looking at her house. They told her to call them back if the lookers actually did something. So Jamie sat there keeping watch. Her oldest son, Eddie, had just gradu-ated high school and started working at Dodge Main. When he came home from his shift at the factory, she told him about the stickup, the shooting, the threat, and the car full of boys casing the house. He called his friend Manny, who said all he had was a .22-caliber Cadet and that he'd bring it over, but they were probably going to need more than just the .22 and the two of them. So Eddie called me and asked to speak to George.

George was my man and had known our family forever. He'd been drafted into the service nearly two years before and was an active Army Ranger squad leader, but he was home on leave. He'd grown up in the neighborhood, and he knew how things were so he treated the threat like any other wartime situation. When he headed over to Aunt Jamie's house, he tried to make me stay home, but they were my family so I went with him.

He called a couple of his buddies, and they came, bringing three rifles and another handgun. They were dressed like anybody else on the streets, T-shirts and jeans, but they held themselves like soldiers. After they sent Jamie upstairs to make sure the kids pulled the mattresses off the beds so they'd be low and away from the windows, the men gathered in the front room to show Eddie and his friend Manny how to use the rifles and to set up a watch schedule. I asked Eddie where he'd found the Puerto Rican *kid*, and he scoffed because he and Manny were around the same age, but he just said, "Round the way." But wherever he'd found him, Manny was game; he'd come strapped, knew how to use his own piece, and he paid attention when George spoke.

With two men posted in front and two in back while George rotated, keeping an eye on the side windows and doors, they kept up the vigil throughout the night. Armed and ready, they held their positions to the left or right of the windows and doors, peering periodically through the curtains. Jamie and I made coffee and sandwiches for them, and after we served them, we sat in the kitchen, where there were no windows, while we waited for the night to end.

Dawn came, and all remained quiet. Relieved and maybe a little disappointed, the warriors relaxed, and after some discussion they decided that if there had been no action that night when heads had been hottest, things would probably blow over. But just the same, George restricted the kids to the backyard and posted one guy at the alley, just in case. They kept up the vigil throughout the day and the rest of the night. But the following morning, George's buddies shook hands with him, Eddie, and Manny and went home. That evening Manny left because he had to go to work. George stayed through the next night, but nothing happened, and eventually he had to head home because his brief leave was ending.

The Plymouth didn't come back, but a couple of months later when the trial was held, all of the boys who'd been in the car showed up. They sat on the prosecutor's side of the courtroom, and Aunt Jamie, Momma, and me sat on the defendant's side, like it was a wedding. Uncle Ronald was charged with attempted murder and carrying a concealed unregistered weapon. He'd been held in the county jail for a few weeks before the family raised enough money for him to make bail so he'd only been out a month or so before he had to come back for the trial.

The boy's family filled the left side of the courtroom. An elderly grandmother and a top-heavy middle-aged mother sat in the front row crying, a damp hanky forever crumpled in her dark fist. The wounded man, who was bandaged to within an inch of his life, leaned heavily on a crutch as he took the stand. He swore he couldn't understand why he'd been shot.

"I didn't even know him. Maybe I bumped into him or something. Said something he didn't like," he admitted. "Hell, I didn't know the man was crazy or that he had a gun until he shot me."

The State-appointed defense attorney had done a little homework. She pointed out that he and his brother had previously been charged with assault and armed robbery and had only been released because the victims had suddenly dropped the charges.

When the skinny guy took the stand, he swore that they'd just come over to look at the baby clothes because his brother's girlfriend had just had a baby, "a little girl named Candy," he added with a smile as he pointed to a girl who sat next to the crying matriarchs. The young woman, who couldn't have been more than sixteen, hugged the sleeping baby, who was swathed in a bundle of pink flannel, to her chest.

Aunt Jamie testified, but the prosecutor pointed out that no gun was found and no money was taken. He accused her of making up the story to protect her brother. And Ronald didn't make it any better because he was angry, angry that he was the one on trial when he'd been protecting his family, angry that the court seemed to be believing the innocent act that the real criminals were putting on.

They found him guilty of the lesser charge. And although the judge didn't seem to believe the fake innocence of the accusers, he sentenced Ronald to two years. He was out in one.

As the deputies cuffed and prepared to take him away, Uncle Ronald turned, winked at Aunt Jamie, who sat in the row of seats just behind him. "No good deed goes unpunished," he said, "but I'd do it again, regardless."

When he got out, and we were all sitting at Aunt Jamie's dining table eating the fried chicken, greens, spaghetti, and pineapple upside-down cake she'd made to celebrate his release, Ronald reared back in his chair, shook his head, and said, "It was bound to happen sometime. Shit just caught up with me." Then he tossed a shot of J&B back, slammed his glass down on the table, and gestured at Eddie to pour him another.

The Runner

he was the prettiest man/I'd ever seen/black, black/blue black/eyes like deep brown shades at half mast

It wasn't that I stopped loving Persia. We had just grown too comfortable, what we had had grown stale. It was still sweet, but like days-old donuts there was a hard, dry undertaste. I'd known Persia practically my whole life. She knew all about how Momma used to turn tricks, and how Daddy used to kick Momma's ass. There were no secrets. She knew me too well. We were weighed down by the past, a past that I knew had formed her image of me. When I was with her, I couldn't step beyond it, couldn't puff out my chest and be that other man; I couldn't pretend. No more surprises. But Marilyn was new.

Say we were talking about the war in Vietnam. I already knew how Persia felt about it. We had talked about it a hundred times, and 90 percent of what she said she had gotten from me. I was always explaining things to her. She liked it that way. She never liked reading, said she liked the way I explained things. So, I always knew what she thought before she said anything. Marilyn was different, always fired up about something she'd seen or read, always reading us lines from her angry poems.

some say his kind are born dead/or at least, dying/black and raggedy/with tight knots that consumed his head/it was a long time before he understood/where he fit/he always knew that he was one of the expendable/and it made his glow special/cause you never knew how long it would last

96

I could feel Marilyn's heat. She was always up in my face trying to shout me down, and I liked it. When Persia and I lived on campus, there was a constant group of folks, mostly fellow students, crowded into the apartment, taking over the living room, the kitchen, and the hallways of the straight-back railroad flat. We would eat, drink, and argue well into the night; it was always hard to get rid of them.

One late night when everyone was curled up in corners or conked out on the rug in front of the fireplace, Marilyn pushed at my knee and said, "You the only one who gives me a run for my money." I leaned back on the sofa and said, "You're always upping your game. When you get going, you're too hot for even me. Somebody needs to hose you down." We both just laughed for a minute, and then all of a sudden she got serious and looked at me with a face full of need.

I knew she liked Persia and wouldn't want to see her hurt. There was never a harsh word between them, and there was always laughing and harmony in our tiny kitchen when they cooked together. They'd even taken a class or two together. I didn't want to hurt Persia either. But there was this burning, this need that just kind of grew between me and Marilyn. I could see it growing in her too, and I wondered if other people could see it. Like the way she started to act when I came into the room. She and Persia could be sitting at the table eating or playing cards, and when I came into the room, Marilyn would drop her fork or misplay a card. Then she'd mumble nervous apologies. Five minutes later, she'd think of a reason to leave the room. I felt guilty too, long before we did anything, and I sort of lost my taste for Persia for a while. We didn't have sex as much, and things she did that I used to think were cute started to annoy the fuck out of me. Like how she relied on me to bring her up to date on what was happening in the world. I used to like how she'd come to me asking me to interpret some shit Kennedy or Nixon had said, and how she would listen real close with her eyes on my face, trying to get it all. Often, she would ask some pretty intuitive questions that made me have to analyze and rethink some of my original conclusions. I used to really get off on that part. But then, when this thing with Marilyn started, those questions started getting on my nerves. The fact that she wouldn't listen to the news or read up on the shit herself started to fuck with me.

lunchtime on the waterfront/just me and george watching/animated sisters filing out of office buildings/coalescing around food vendors/ trucks and three-wheeled wagons/the smell of hot dogs and tamales/ the sound of the river lashing against the shore/and george laughing at brothers in round wire-rimmed glasses and wing tips/sisters pretending not to notice being noticed/those hips george would say should be holding babies not straining the buttons of business suits

Sunday. I remember because the buses weren't running right. We had already had dinner, and it was getting late. Marilyn said she couldn't stay over because she had some studying or something to do so Persia asked me to take her home. I asked Persia if she wanted to come with us. She said she wanted to straighten up a little so she told me to go on. If she hadn't done that, maybe? Maybe it was supposed to happen like that. See, I figured it would just pass, you know the feeling, but with Marilyn just there, sitting next to me in the front seat, and us alone like that, I don't know. When we drove up in front of her house, she leaned close to me, and I could feel her nipples, all hard and shit, rubbing against my arm. Then she reached up and kissed me. What was I supposed to do? So, I followed her into her house, and when I got home Persia was already asleep so I didn't even have to make up a lie.

his body was smooth/no hair/just the soft wool on his head/and the crinkly curls at his sex/when he came/there was pain on his face/ a twisted bliss/and I fell deeper

After that, it seemed like I was always angry at Persia. She was always around, always in my fucking face. Maybe it was guilt, but then I couldn't see clearly. A couple of times, I almost told her about me and Marilyn. When I started to, it wouldn't come out. Maybe I didn't want to crush her. Maybe I didn't want to lose her. All I know is that when I felt like I wanted to come clean, I would treat her nice for a while, take her out or cook for her, and we'd talk about something in the news that she'd been bugging me about.

eyes like deep-brown shades/at half-mast/voice like a cello

I don't know when it happened, but one day I got tired of sneaking out. I got tired of the innuendos and the way Marilyn always found a reason to touch me when other people were around. And then she began to want more. She wanted more time; she'd complain that we weren't able to show our feelings in public, and she'd ask whether I still loved Persia. When she thought no one was looking, she'd give me these sad faces, and I'd feel bad and angry and afraid that somebody might see. After a while, it all became too much.

and he could run/so fast/that I/could never catch him

George and Persia

Last night, night before
Twenty-four robbers at my door,
I got up and let 'em in
Hit 'em in the head with a rollin pin.

George would be leaning up against the big elm tree in front of our house, singing out the rhyme and pressing his eyes hard into his forearm. You could be sure that George wouldn't peek. That's one of the things I always liked about him: you could trust him. If he said he was going to do something, it was as good as done.

In the summertime, our mommas would sit on the porch and watch us play. When they were in a good mood, they'd let us play way past the time when the streetlights came on.

I was a couple of years older than George, and in those days that was a lot. Even though I knew George liked me, I wouldn't have nothing to do with him cause he was a *baby*. Once when we were playing hide-and-seek, George decided to turn it into a game of hide-and-go-get-it. I was hiding behind the house just under the stairs. When he found me, he didn't holler out like he was supposed to. He stood there looking at me for a minute, and then he took my hand and helped me up. Once I was steady on my feet, he pulled me to him and kissed me on the neck like he was a man. I liked the feel of his body, the closeness. I liked him, but I couldn't let him touch me like that. I thought about him being just a baby and me being the oldest. So, I pushed him away hard and whispered, "Boy, if you don't get away from me, I'm gon slap the black off you."

Miss Belle, you want me to help you in there with some of that? . . . Oh, I'm OK. Your table looks really good. You got enough food in there to feed an army. George would be proud.

I was twelve then, and George was about ten. I remember him standing there in those raggedy gym shoes and too-short khakis. He looked embarrassed, then angry, but only for a minute. Then he nodded, as if to say, "OK," and he stretched his hand out, tagged me, and then ran off. Since then, a lot of things have happened.

In high school, me and George got to be good friends. He skipped a grade; he was really smart. So when I was a senior, he was a junior. He was always older than his years anyway. I used to tell him everything and ask what he thought I should do. He gave good advice too.

I remember once, we were sitting at the back of the auditorium watching the tryouts for the Christmas talent show. It was mostly boys imitating the Temptations or girl groups singing "Baby Love." But there was this one modern dance group dancing to Dexter Gordon's version of "Take the A Train." You know how he slows it down and makes it sort of sensual? Well, the music got really soft as the lead dancer moved upstage, making seductive pelvic movements while the other dancers lunged at her like they wanted to touch her but couldn't. George looked like he was really into it. Anyway, that was when I decided to tell him I wanted to get rid of my virginity.

He looked at me real funny and seemed to forget all about the dancers, so I told him who I wanted to give it to and why. He didn't like the boy cause he was a lot older than us. The guy was a senior, still in high school, and twenty-two years old. I felt like I had to defend the guy so I explained that the guy was from down south and had to work in the fields instead of going to school. George said he didn't like the guy cause he thought he was a player and already had too many women. Then he asked why I was in such a rush? I told him I wanted to see what it was like and figured it would be best to do it with somebody old enough to know what he was doing.

"But do you love him?" George had asked.

I should have listened to George, but I was young.

You know, George was my first real lover. He taught me what it was like to touch and feel and be with someone you love, but that was a few years later.

We started staying together about a year after he graduated from high school. We got this apartment over on Canfield. Now it's a historic district, but then it was just a bunch of old houses that had been turned into apartments. The rent was only $160 a month. Can you believe that? And we had two bedrooms *and* a fireplace. We had scholarships and work-study jobs. It was '69, and the government was trying to make amends for four hundred years of slavery. Yeah, I know, feeble attempt, but it's a lot better than what they *ain't* doing now. George was majoring in econ; I was considering art history.

We always had a house full of folks arguing about Stonewall, or whether the money our government invested in the space program was worth it, or why we were really in Vietnam. The sounds of Stevie, War, or the Last Poets filled the room, and we'd be sipping Boone's Farm or Lambrusco. There was a chess board set up in front of the fireplace, and there was always a couple of folks bent over it in battle

I taught George to play, but he quickly outclassed me once he learned the basics. We kept the fireplace fed with old newspaper and broken furniture that we found in the alley. And there was usually a big iron pot of navy beans or greens and ham hocks or black-eyed peas on the stove in the kitchen. George was a good cook, but he always made me cook the cornbread because he said I put just the right amount of sugar in it. Sometimes we'd fry up a batch of chicken wings, or one of the sisters would bring over a tray of macaroni and cheese or some candied yams. It was catch as catch can because we never had much money.

Those were some good times . . . cause George was there. When I would get tired of the folks or school . . . or life, I could just take George by the hand and head down that long hall to the back room. We didn't have a bed, just a mattress and box spring, but I kept fresh linen on it, and we'd stretch out next to each other, and he'd pull me into his arms and hold me. I'd lay there with my head on his chest, listening to his heart.

There were some rough times. Like the time . . . See, I'm jealous, and it doesn't take much to tick me off. I used to have this friend. Her name was Marilyn, I mean we were tight. We used to go window-shopping, and sometimes she'd drag me out to a party or something without George. Mostly, we studied together. She'd come over to the house and sit up arguing with the rest of the folks about who was right, Martin or Malcolm, predicting the outcome of the revolution in Mozambique, or laughing at that fool, Nixon.

I remember when I found out that she and George had a thing. I was pissed! I wanted to kill somebody. But it was my fault. Like my momma used to say, never tell a woman how good your man is because she bound to want to try him out.

George denied everything, and this witch come telling me how she loved George and was going to continue seeing him if he was willing. I banished her from my house and my life, and George had hell to pay for months after that. Every chance I got, I'd throw it up in his face. He would be trying to make normal conversation at dinner, and I'd find some way to bring the conversation back around to Marilyn. It was like I had a hole in me that was infected, and the right antibiotic hadn't been discovered.

Sometimes, we'd be in bed, and he'd come up behind me and try to spoon. I'd pull away from him and draw my knees up to my chest. He hated it when I slept like that cause he couldn't get near me. He used to say that I was trying to puncture him with my bony knees and elbows. But he started being his old sweet self again, and he must have been coaching his friends.

They kept whispering in my ear about how I know George ain't never loved nobody but me, and how Marilyn wasn't nothing but a piece of tail. Whatever. I bought it and I felt a lot better when I did.

Stella, fix me a drink too. Hey, here's my glass. A Cuba Libre, *por favor* . . . Girl, that's just rum and Coke . . . Thanks, I'll do the same for you sometime.

Too bad he never got his degree. He dropped out to work at Fleetwood because his stepdaddy died and somebody had to pay his momma's rent. Leaving school was really hard for him, and he really hated the plant. Every night he would come home whipped. Most of the time, he'd just plop down in the first chair he'd come to. He'd sit there an hour or more before he could get up enough strength to undress and take a shower. He complained all the time about how the place had no windows, how boring it was to be a cog on the line, and how he hated that cracker foreman and his clipboard. Sometimes he'd go in and then he would have me call the factory with an emergency so he'd get in a few hours, make some money, but he wouldn't have to work a whole day.

And then, well, he got drafted . . . He only had two months to go, and I thought the goddamn war was supposed to be over. The day we heard, I had just gotten a letter from him. It was a thick one, so full of promises. I was so happy.

I didn't think I could go into that church today. I lay awake all last night thinking about the plans we had made for when he got home. I couldn't stand to see him lying there in that fucking box, his face all dull and pasty.

I didn't want to come off like one of those church sisters that get the Holy Ghost and fall all out in the aisle, but I just couldn't contain the grief. You saw how long I sat there before I got up the courage to view his body. But when I saw him lying there, sleep-like, I wanted to climb up in there and lay my head on his chest and listen to his heart, to feel it beating against my cheek.

I didn't mean to mess up the flowers. I just wanted to touch him . . . to be near him one more time.

Hand me one of those Kleenex. Thanks. Oh, I'm alright, Miss Belle. Really. How you holding up? . . . Can I get a hug? I think George would want his two main ladies to be there for each other.

With "Fixing a Hole" from the Beatles'
Sgt. Pepper's Lonely Hearts Club Band in mind . . .

Belle Fixes a Hole

She'd been going to this church for a few months now. At first, it was just Sunday afternoons, the one o'clock service. After a while, she started going to Saturday morning Bible study, and then Wednesday night prayer meetings. It was a good-sized church, not one of those clapboard storefronts with nine members including the preacher. Belle had been raised in bantam churches with self-taught preachers who held their mostly female congregations together with thunder-voiced fire-and-brimstone sermons, jackleg preachers who dangled the promise of comfort while doling out fear. But Belle was older now, and she needed something different.

This new church had a dark cherrywood pulpit and altar and oak pews, a far cry from the folding chairs and collapsible table she'd endured in those storefront churches. The stained-glass windows on either side of the sanctuary were tall, arched, brightly colored, and showed Jesus with a flock of sheep on one side and him dragging his cross on his back on the other. It wasn't the fact that everything looked expensive. The cost of things didn't impress Belle; she prided herself on being a practical woman. It was just that the windows and the altar gave the place substance, made it feel reliable.

But it was the sign on the front lawn that had captured her. The red-brick-and-glass marquee looked like a monument or a headstone. Bold black letters proclaimed the New Jerusalem, COGIC, and just below, in smaller letters, it said, "Be not afraid, for I am with thee." Isaiah 41:10. Later she learned that the verse changed every week.

But the first day she noticed it, she was coming back from the cemetery. It was a gray, rainy day, and the bus had stopped to let a passenger off so she'd had time to read the sign. She felt the chill of those words all the way down to the small of her back. The next day, she got off the bus to get a better look at the whole thing: the sign, the big brick building, the healthy grass and the nice neat way it had been cut. It was a long ways away from the poster board with letters scrawled in house paint nailed above the storefront's door and the plastic curtains that covered the display windows in the churches she'd grown up in.

In the beginning, Belle sat in the back, in the far corner of New Jerusalem's last row. She would turn her body toward the open double doors, her arm stretched along the back of the pew as she watched people flow into the sanctuary. Some would stand in the doorway and look around before deciding where to sit. Others headed straight to a favored seat without stopping. Sometimes a smiling husband, wife, or friend scooted over to make room.

Weeks passed, and Belle continued to watch the procession of parishioners file into the sanctuary. She began to anticipate the swell of cliques as they gathered, first one well-dressed woman in a large-brimmed or silk-flower-topped hat, then another, drawn together like paper clips to a magnet before they moved en masse to their chosen pew. After a while, she could predict where each person or group would sit. The women with husbands would sit in the center pews near the front. Younger women with children sat in the back near the doors; while widows and otherwise older single women sat in the left pew nearest the preacher.

The last group was a lively cluster of brightly colored, big flowered hats and cardboard fans that fluttered as the women nodded and shouted Amen to draw the preacher's eye and let him know they were listening. When the choir got really good or the preacher's sermon got especially heated, one of the flowers would begin nodding fitfully just before it jumped up and did a little joy dance. The Holy Ghost had the tendency to move a body, and sometimes it was catching. Sometimes it would catch hold of a whole handful of sisters all at once. When that happened, the shouting and jumping would light up the church. So joined to the spirit, some sisters would get feverish and swoon or faint. Ushers, calm women in white nurses' uniforms, gloves, and thick orthopedic shoes, and deacons, men in dark suits, would rush over to soothe or escort the fallen woman back to her bench or downstairs to the infirmary. The fur-coated married women would press their lips together and shake their heads. Belle just grinned and enjoyed the show.

Although Belle had been raised in the church, she didn't know whether she really believed. Sometimes she read Psalms when she needed comfort, but she favored a cold beer in a loud bar. Nowadays, though, neither seemed to work. One morning she looked into the bathroom mirror as she was washing her face and saw bags forming under her eyes. They were not the kind that came from losing sleep after a night out; these were deep set, and the skin around her mouth seemed slack like it wanted to droop. Every morning she had to drag herself out of bed, and the weariness seemed to grow. She knew she had to do something.

She didn't have the heart for drinking and partying like she used to. Besides, the bars were filled with young girls, and with them around, even the men Belle's age wouldn't give her the time of day. And the church had taken much more than it had given. But, when the end time came, she wanted a proper funeral, and that meant finding a church home. It wasn't something she looked forward to; it was something she felt she had to do, like paying the gas or electric bill.

When she first started going to New Jerusalem, she sat near the door ready to bolt because she was afraid someone would recognize her for the fraud she was, but the more she attended, the less fear she felt. Now when she walked through its wide double doors, she felt a sense of release like a horse must feel when the groom eases the bit out of its mouth. And the music was glorious; the youth choir could make you cry. Then there were the women in the left pew; they always seemed to be having a good time.

As a child, she spent long hours kneeling next to her momma in prayer, but deep down Belle saw the whole thing as a scam, a way to control people and beat them out of their money. Heaven and hell, ambrosia, scalding pits, Jesus and Judas and Job and his boils—she'd always liked the stories. They were full of colorful characters and lessons. She'd used them on her own kids when they were growing up. But even when she was younger and more vulnerable, the spirit never touched her, and the stories seemed like fairy tales. There wasn't much difference between Job and Cinderella or Sleeping Beauty. Sometimes life was hard, and sometimes it got better, but even the better never stayed that way. Who knew what happened to Cinderella or Sleeping Beauty or even Job after the words in the book stopped.

But now Belle wanted it to touch her. She wanted something to touch her, because for a long time now she had felt nothing. The numbing began when she lost her oldest son. It had felt like being sliced in half, but it had lessened because there was still hope. When she lost her youngest daughter, Cassandra, the one she'd had time to hold close and give her true self to, Belle wondered if the vengeful God that her mother and those jackleg preachers spoke of really existed. She wondered if He had taken her baby to make her suffer. She feared that He was paying her back for all the wrong she had done, for all the men she had slept with, for the babies she had without benefit of marriage, for long nights spent in bars drinking and living fast, for not believing in Him.

After Cassandra died, there had been years of misery. Too often, she woke up to a room without air, and she couldn't breathe or swallow. When she finally caught her breath and remembered the loss, she couldn't stop crying. They tried to calm her, the other kids and Michael, who was her last man friend. But nothing they did helped. Time. Time passed, and the memories blurred. The feelings turned to a stone that burrowed deep into her gut. It pained her every so often, vibrating through her body, causing even her teeth to hurt, but time dulled even that, and then there was nothing. By then, the other kids had gone off to live their own lives, and Michael had just gone.

The music felt good. "Rock of a—ges, cleft for me/Let me hide my—self in Thee." It swelled up in her, and she hummed along as the choir rocked back and forth, their voices pushing the notes. A shiver raced up her spine, and she could feel tears filling her eyes. "Let the wa—ter and the blood/From Thy wound—ed side which flowed." The rhythm washed over her as she mouthed the words, a song of prayer. "Be of sin the dou—ble cure/Save from wrath and make me pure." Eyes closed and right hand raised high above her head, waving with the flow of the music, she testified to Him, owning her need.

The preacher, a tall dark-skinned middle-aged man in a black robe with a wide purple stole trimmed in bright gold, stepped up to the pulpit. He was a good-looking man with a full, round voice. His words were measured as though he was considering their meaning as he spoke. The ladies in the left pew got quiet, their eyes directed at the pulpit, the man, and the voice. Even the married couples hushed and looked up to receive the Word.

"Some say that Mary Magdalene is a much maligned woman. That she was a victim, not only of her time, but of the church." The minister's voice took on a singsong cadence, the timbre getting deeper as he warmed to his story. "Some say that she was an apostle and that because she was a woman her words were dismissed, her contribution to our faith hidden and her person vilified. Others say that she was an adulterer and a prostitute who came to Jesus for forgiveness. Whatever the case, *we* can learn from her faith, from her actions. Turn to Luke, chapter seven, verse thirty-six."

There was a bump and flutter as the congregation pulled out Bibles and leafed through the thin pages. The flutter settled, and then there was silence as they waited to be led.

"Now one of the Pharisees asked Jesus to have dinner with him," the preacher said before he began to read from the Book. "And he went into the Pharisee's house, and sat down to meat. And behold, a woman in the city, who was a sinner, when she found that Jesus dined in the Pharisee's house, she brought an alabaster box of ointment and stood at his feet weeping, and began to wash his feet with tears, and did dry them with the hairs of her head, and kissed his feet, and anointed them with the ointment." The minister pulled a handkerchief from his sleeve, wiped his forehead, and looked out into the audience.

"Now that Pharisee asked Jesus, 'Do you know who that woman is that you let touch you?' And Jesus answered him with a *question*." The preacher did a little jump to punctuate his statement.

"He asked Simon, the Pharisee, if one man owed five hundred dollars and another owed fifty to a moneylender who forgave both debts, which would love him more? And Simon said, 'Why, the one with the larger debts.'" The church waited as though it hadn't heard this story a hundred times before. The preacher stood back, hands clasping the sides of his stole as he smiled at his audience and nodded with the benevolence of the Savior. "And Jesus said, 'That's right, Simon.'" The crowd breathed and smiled back; a scattered chorus of Amens came from the pews. The minister grinned out at his congregation.

"And then he let Simon have it. He said, 'See thou this woman. I came to your house, and you gave me no water for my feet. You gave me no kiss. My head you did not anoint with oil, but this woman washed my feet with her tears and hath not ceased to kiss my feet.'" The preacher was jumping, a little bounce on his toes as he rose to the Word, feeling the exaltation of the tale.

"He looked at Mary Magdalene, who had been maligned by this man, and he saw the love and faith and the possibility of joy that radiated from her soul." The tall, beautiful man in the long robe began to read from the Scripture again. "'Wherefore I say unto thee, her sins, which are many, are forgiven; for she loved much . . . And he said unto her, thy sins are forgiven . . . Thy faith hath saved thee; go in peace.'" A chorus of Amens filled the church, and a refrain of "Thank you, Jesus," rang out from the left pew. "Let us pray," the preacher said as he closed the Book.

The choir sang "Blessed Assurance," and Belle found it difficult to sing along. Her throat was clogged with tears, but she joined in the refrain: "This is my sto—ry, this is my song, praising my Sav—ior all the day long." Head bowed, she leaned back into the solid wood of the pew and let the tears flow.

When the altar call began and the choir began its somber song, Belle watched the straggling stream of sinners make their way to the front of the church. The beautiful man looked out over the congregation. "You need not bear the burden alone," he said, and Belle felt like he was looking right at her, the light in his eyes pulling, drawing her forward. "Have you ever been blessed? Have you ever longed for sweet rest?" He spoke quietly, his voice keeping time to the rhythms of the choir as they sang, "Come to Jesus. Come to Jesus. Come to Jesus just now. He will save you. He will save you. He will save you just now."

Belle nodded and stood. She gripped the edge of the pew in front of her, the oak solid beneath her fingers. "No sin is too great," the pastor said to her. "Give your cares to Jesus. Give your soul to Jesus. He won't let you down." Belle slipped into the aisle and made her way to the altar, where she knelt and bowed her head. "He will hear you. He will hear you," the choir sang, and Belle released the breath that she had been holding for so long.

She bowed her head, welcoming the weight and warmth of the preacher's large hand when it came to rest on her head. As he prayed, Belle felt something rise up in her, something warm like love, and she knew she wanted to give it to God. The choir rose, the rustle of their robes like a flock of birds released, their voices rejoicing as they sang, "God is—so good to me, God is so good to me." The rhythm of their swelling voices rushed through Belle as she stood, hand raised to God and feet doing a hop-skip dance to the beat of her joy.

Luz in Progress

I'm lying here on my stomach, legs stretched the length of the yellow Formica dinner table. My feet don't quite reach the end. I rest my chin on my hands and press my fingers into the cold, hard surface. It feels clean and safe up here. I'm being really quiet. He never shouts at me to get off the table, and if I'm really quiet he ignores me and lets me listen. He is practicing one of his songs while he gets his outfit ready for tonight's show. The song is soft-like and really pretty. Torch song, he calls it. I watch him through my eyelashes so he won't see me watching. He already knows I'm listening.

He has on a black bustier with little white threads running all through it and a matching thong that pushes his stuff out in front and shows the smooth line of his butt in the back. The skin looks so smooth and clean and soft that I want to touch it. As he comes closer, singing his soft, sad song, I just reach out little by little and run my hand down the length of the closest butt cheek. He swats at the place I touched like he's fanning at a fly, but when he sees it was me he just smirks, shakes his head, and keeps smoothing out the long dress because he knows I'm just a kid and it don't mean nothing. The skin is cool and firm and feels really nice. Without opening my eyes any wider, I stroke it once more, and then I just pull my arm back to my side. When he finishes his song and the sparkly dress is falling nicely from its hanger, he stands there looking down at me. I open my eyes and wait.

"You know, Luz," he says to me, "that place Manolo goes to ain't a real job. He turns tricks." And then he just picks up his little black cotton kimono with the fuchsia birds on the back and pulls it on. I look at him. I'm only eight and a girl, but I know what turning tricks is, and my brother Manny don't do it. He is a man; he ain't no fag like Estrella here, who dresses up like a lady and sings in a bar. Manny is a man with muscles on both his arms, who can still pick me up, and who pays the rent and buys food when Mami spends the check getting high or don't come home.

I look at Estrella, who is bending over by the refrigerator, pulling out a beer. I want to spit on that lying punk. I'm sitting up now and I'm mad, wondering why he'd say something out of the blue like that about Manny. I want to ask him why, but instead I say, "Manny says fags always think everybody is like them."

"*Te dijo*, Luz," he says to me. "I ain't no fag. I'm a cross-dresser. I like to wear women's clothes. They make me feel the part. Make me sing better."

"Fag," I taunt.

"I like women," he pouts. "You know Lupita *es mi novia*."

"Why you want to say that about Manny?" I have to ask.

"Cause it's true."

"I thought you were my friend." One tear; I'm not crying.

"I am. Want something to drink? *¿Tienes hambre?*" he asks.

"I don't want your nasty food." I'm down off the table and headed toward the door.

"Where you gonna go, Luz? Your mami's not home, and Manny's probably trying to get some sleep before work," he says, pulling some stuff out of the fridge.

"Why you say that bout Manny?"

"I thought you should know so when your little friends at school or somebody from the neighborhood throws it at you, you'll be ready for 'em."

I stand there for a long time, not saying nothing.

"That *pendejo* Carlito, Julio's brother, saw Manny in the back room with a client last night," Estrella says.

Watching him put sandwiches together and warm the milk for the coffee, I think how it is suddenly cold in Estrella's stuffy little apartment.

"Come on over here and talk to me." But he's not looking at me. He keeps his eyes on what he's doing. I don't move.

He stands there with the plates in his hands, looking really tall in the kimono that barely comes to the bottom of his hips. Wiry black hairs curl just inside the front of his bustier. He puts the plates down on the table.

"I'll make you some coffee with lots of milk and sugar. Just like you like it. Sit down."

I watch him moving back and forth between the little kitchen place and the table.

"Manny ain't no fag," I say.

"I didn't say he was, Luz." He sets the coffee down. "Come on."

He sits down in the chair on the other side of the table and waits for me. Finally, I move over to the table and take a seat across from him. We bow our heads, make temples of our hands, and he says grace.

"Heavenly Father," he begins.

I'm thinking, *Please don't let Manny be no fag.*

He's asking that the food be blessed, and I'm telling God I don't care about the food, just make what Estrella said about Manny be a lie. He finishes, and I still have my eyes closed.

When I open my eyes, he has picked up his sandwich and is opening it and looking it over like he hadn't just made it himself.

"It's not the worst thing in the world, Luz. He's real careful. They wear rubbers so he don't catch nothing." He puts his sandwich back together and bites it.

"Drink your coffee," he says to me and puts the cup in front of me.

I lean down low over it and, without picking it up, put my mouth on the rim of the cup and sip. It's really full, and the liquid is hot and sweet, just like I like it.

"You know Manny is a good-looking man. Those big, dark eyes and all that sandy hair. He can make a lot of money." He takes another bite.

"Manny ain't no man yet," I say. "He's only seventeen."

"He's the man in your house. With your mami strung out like that, don't no other money come in. She smokes up what little the State sends."

I'm going to cry if he keeps talking, so I keep staring at the beige liquid like it's got an answer.

"Manny loves you, Luz. Not saying he doing it just for you, cause he gotta eat and sleep too, but—" Stopping all of a sudden, like he ran out of words. He takes a sip of his beer to cover up, and it's quiet for a long while.

I watch a tear drop into my coffee.

"How did it happen?" I ask.

He looks at me, and I can see a tender, little smile in his eyes like he saying, "I knew I could trust you."

"He didn't want to sell drugs with the Counts, what with your mami and all, and bussing tables don't pay nothing, and the guys at the club kept asking him. So, one day he just did it."

He watches me awhile, and then he says, "Luz, it's not right. And he would never want you to have to do something like that. In fact, that's one of the reasons he does it. So you won't have to. But Luz, don't hate him, and don't make him feel worse about himself than he already does."

I look up at him, and by now I'm really crying. I nod in agreement, and he holds out his arms. I run around the table and press my face into the stiff stays of his bustier as he brushes my hair with his hand.

"It's only a temporary thing, Luz. Manolo's smart, a survivor. He'll come up with something better before you know it."

La Bruja

The old woman mumbled curses as she circled the house, and every so often she bent over, scooped up a handful of grassy dirt and gravel, and threw it at the house. It sounded like rain as it bounced off the doors and windows. Then she'd spit and mumble, incoherent sounds that rose and fell like an ancient chant. Her mouth must have run dry because the spitting was ceremonial; only the occasional droplet sputtered from her lips. Her two sons, dressed in faded, ill-shaped T-shirts and sagging jeans, stood like scowling sentinels on either side of the gate, watching the house. Migdalia, or Dalia, as everyone at school called her, and I squatted in the living room peeking out from behind the dusty curtains. Lucinda, my stepmother, was posted in the back bedroom at the window, where she watched *la bruja* as she cursed and spit her way around the back of the house. Ours was a good-sized house on the corner with a wide yard around it.

Papi was at work, the afternoon shift, and he wouldn't be home for another hour. It was nearly eight o'clock, but it was still light outside. July was one of the longest, warmest months of the year, and it wouldn't get dark until after nine. With all the windows and doors shut tight, the house was getting really hot and stuffy. The heat from the stove didn't help, and the heavy garlic and olive oil that Lucinda used to make the rice seasoned the air.

"Maybe we should call the police," Dalia said as she sat heavily on her bottom, resting the back of her head against the curtain-covered windowsill.

"What are we gonna say? There's a voodoo lady outside who's putting a spell on our house?" I asked.

Dalia nodded.

I smirked. "Yeah, that's sure to get them over here. Besides, you're liable to be in more trouble than them if the cops come."

"I'm scared," she said.

"If they were going to do something real, they would have done it by now," I said, peeking out again. The old woman had made it back around to the front of the house.

"Like what?" she asked.

I shrugged. "I don't know. Maybe breaking a window or knocking the door down."

Dalia's eyes got big.

"But see, they're just standing out there, and that bruja is just putting a pretend spell on us."

"What if it's real? What if what she says is real?" Dalia asked. "That darkness will cover us and all we do will fail."

"She ain't no real obeah woman," I said. "She's just trying to scare us. Trying to get us to give in."

"How do you know?" Dalia asked.

I didn't say anything; I just peeked out again. "She's just an old lady," I said as the wild-haired woman in the snap-front flowered housecoat and fake-leather men's slippers threw a handful of dirt at me. The tiny pellets sounded like an ice storm as they hit the glass and rained down the window.

She said something to her sons, and one of them nodded. They were just regular guys in jeans and oversized T-shirts. Neither was particularly big or muscular. They were just normal, dark hair and sun-browned skin. If I'd just seen them around the neighborhood, I wouldn't have looked twice. Neither was particularly *guapo o feo*. But standing there with scowls on their faces, one with his arms crossed and the other with that sketchy mustache, they looked mean. *El bigote's* eyes caught mine, and he lifted his chin at me, a quick, glaring jut. Stunned, I closed the curtain and slid down next to Dalia.

The baby started to cry, and Dalia moved to get up.

"I've got her," Lucinda said from the back room.

Dalia plopped back down.

"I'm sorry," she said.

"It's OK," I said.

She didn't say anything else, but I could see the tears dampening her cheeks. I pulled her into a hug.

"I didn't have any place else to go."

"I know," I said.

"I couldn't take the baby to mami's house."

I nodded. She pulled back, trying to see my face.

"Mami's real sick, and I couldn't risk the baby getting sick too." Her eyes were red.

"I know," I said, nodding because I really did. Her mother was frail, had been suffering from tuberculosis for a while. She was surely dying. Her two youngest daughters were in foster care. At fifteen and pregnant, Dalia had been allowed to stay at home and care for her mother, and then Dalia had been arrested for shoplifting. While serving her six-month term in the Wayne County Juvenile Detention Center, she gave birth to a baby girl. When she refused to put the baby up for adoption, they put the newborn in foster care.

"You just went over there and took her?" I asked, marveling at her bravery.

She grinned back at me. "Yeah. She was in there all by herself in the middle of the bed. Her diaper was soaked like it hadn't been changed all day. She was asleep, but her face was all red like maybe she had cried herself to sleep.

"I just walked right in; the screen door wasn't even locked. The bruja was in the kitchen weighing out dime bags, and a couple of little kids, probably her other foster kids, were watching cartoons in the living room. The baby was in the bedroom right off the front room.

"Anyway, I found a diaper, changed her, and wrapped her in a blanket. Then I held her for a minute, just rocking her. After a minute or two, I picked up the half-empty bottle of milk that had rolled onto the floor, grabbed a handful of diapers, and just walked out with her."

I shook my head at her nerve.

"I couldn't leave her there like that," she insisted.

"Nobody said anything?" I asked.

"There wasn't anybody around to say anything. The kids watching TV didn't even look up when I slipped out the door. Who knows how long she'd been lying there like that?"

When Lucinda brought the baby into the room, it had quieted and was wrapped tightly in the little flannel blanket with the pink-and-yellow circus animals that I'd bought her when we were planning to give Dalia a baby shower.

"I changed her diaper. Here," Lucinda said as she handed the bundle to Dalia. "I'll fix her a bottle."

"Thanks," Dalia said as she rocked the bundle and Lucinda padded toward the kitchen.

A clod of dirt hit the front door, broke into pieces, and fell heavily onto the wooden planks of the porch like a burst of hail. At the sudden sound, the baby gave a tiny, startled cry. Dalia and I stared at the front door before moving away from it and the window nearest it. She hugged the baby close, bouncing it gently and patting its bottom. Then she smiled down at the tiny bundle. I couldn't imagine having such a responsibility.

Just last year, Dalia was just like me. Her mother was sick, but she wasn't as bad then, and she encouraged Dalia to go to Homecoming. She told her she still remembered hers, and it was one of the best days of her life. To earn the money for our dresses, we stood in front of the neighborhood supermarket passing out leaflets that advertised legal services and a dental clinic. After school for nearly two months, we handed out those fliers, but it was OK because we did it together, and we earned enough to pay for our dresses.

I envied the way she looked in the blue matte satin dress she bought, so posh. She was the pretty one, the one that basketball players asked out. I was the slightly chubby friend, the cock blocker, but we were inseparable. Well, most of the time. She was a good friend; I'd known her since before kindergarten, and she'd always been there for me.

"Did you give her a name?" I asked.

She shook her head. "They took her away so fast, but I wanted to call her Vita."

There was a commotion outside, raised voices, feet shuffling on packed dirt. I thought I heard Papi's voice so I went back to the window and peeked through the curtain. The neighbors across the street, Mrs. Lopez, her brother, and her son and daughter in-law, had gathered on their porch and were watching our house. One of the bruja's sons was holding the wooden box that Papi had built to hold the chicks. Lucinda kept a coop out back with a handful of chickens, and recently a few chicks had hatched. They were plump, bright-yellow balls of down.

I could hear Papi's voice. He was on the porch, but I couldn't see him from where I sat. Finally, he moved, and I could see his blue work uniform; oil from the car parts he'd been lifting at the plant stained his pants. I knew how he liked to come home to quiet and take a bath before having his dinner. I felt sorry that he had to come home to all of this, but I was glad to see him.

He started down the steps, moving toward the guy with the box. *"¡Cabrón! ¿Quieres morir?"* he shouted. The bruja grabbed one of the chicks from the box and threw it at Papi. It sailed past him and landed on the porch. I ran to the door, opened it, and stepped out onto the porch. There was no way that I was going to leave my papi out there alone with those crazies.

Papi lunged toward the man with the box, but the guy danced around, holding the box just out of Papi's reach. By then, the bruja had grabbed another chick and threw it at Dalia, who was peeking out from behind the curtains with the baby in her arms.

The chick bounced off the window and landed on the porch a few feet from its brother. The bruja's other son was grabbing at Papi, but Papi shook him off, twisted around, and punched him in the face. The younger man fell to the ground, howling and clutching his nose. His mother screamed, "You greasy *culero*!" She jumped onto Papi's back and started pulling his hair and pounding his shoulders with her fists. I was down the steps and running toward the bruja, but Papi had shaken her off. She had fallen on her backside and was yelling, "You evil man." Then she was up and standing in a crouch, like a wrestler trying to block the path that led to our steps. "Give us back the baby," she shouted as she pranced around in front of Papi, looking pretty scary as she tried to block his way.

Papi pushed her to the side and dashed into the house. I'd left the door wide open, and now Lucinda was standing on the porch. Suddenly Papi was standing next to Lucinda cocking his hunting rifle. He aimed it at the man holding the box of chicks.

"Put the box down gently and leave," Papi said.

The man's eyes got big, but he set the box down on the ground, extra slowly.

"We just want the baby back," the man said after he'd straightened up and taken a step back.

"That's not going to happen," Papi said. He looked back at Dalia standing in the window holding her baby, then at Lucinda standing on the porch, and then at me standing in the yard.

"Get back in the house," he said to me.

"I'll call the cops. All of you will go to jail," the bruja yelled.

"If you could do that, you would've called them already."

"Bad luck will follow you," the bruja said, twisting two forked fingers at Papi and giving him the evil eye as she bent to help her son up.

"That may be," Papi said, "but right now, you and your sons will be leaving. You are trespassing, and worse, you're threatening my family. Leave. Now."

"*Mija*," he said to me. "Get—in—the—house." He said it slow and soft, and I knew he meant right now.

The bruja spewed more curses, and her sons shouted foul names at Papi. I scrambled back into the house. By the time I squeezed in next to Dalia at the window, they were backing away. *El bigote* was holding his jaw, and *la bruja* was soothing him, rubbing a hand across his back. The other one was snarling and cursing, but they were leaving.

Papi put the rifle away, Lucinda retrieved the box of chickens, and I scooped the fallen chicks up off the porch. Across the street, the neighbors who had gathered for the show were beginning to melt away.

We took the chicks into the kitchen, and we all sat around the table explaining about Dalia and the baby while Papi looked over the injured chicks, applying Scotch tape to the split belly of one and dusting them both off with a damp cloth. Papi listened, nodded, and asked a question when he needed more information. As she told her story, Dalia and then the baby began to cry. When she realized that her crying was upsetting the baby, she stopped, sniffed back her tears, and began bouncing the baby on her hip. Lucinda set a hot cup of creamy coffee in front of Papi. He sipped it, nodded, and then drank a bit more. Then he asked Dalia a couple more questions, and Lucinda handed Dalia a bottle for the baby. Papi drank his coffee, and Dalia sat across the table from Papi with the contented baby in her lap sucking greedily at the warm bottle. The chicks were resting in their box, which I put on the floor next to the back door.

"I'll talk to them tomorrow," Papi said. "They can get more foster kids. It'll be a lot easier for them to do that if they work with us to help you keep yours. They've got too many things going on over there to risk it all for one baby."

"Can Dalia stay with us?" I asked.

Papi looked at Lucinda, who nodded.

"For now," he said thoughtfully. "We'll have to talk to her social worker to get things straightened out, but we'll see how it goes. Look, I'm going to take my bath now," he added as he scooted his chair back from the table and headed toward his and Lucinda's bedroom.

I took Papi's cup over to the sink and washed and rinsed it before setting it on the dish rack to dry.

Manny

"Hey, Manny." It was Diesel. He stood in the doorway that separated the club from the kitchen. This far back, the music was a low drone, a relentless beat that felt like it had crawled under the floorboards.

Manny didn't turn around. He took another drag from his cigarette. "Diesel," he acknowledged as he blew the smoke out. Manny had come into the kitchen to catch his breath. It was closed, and he knew that the staff would have long since cleaned up and gone home.

"You shoulda seen Ma today," Diesel half laughed. "She was on blast, full-on wicked witch of the Southwest."

Manny half laughed too, a grunt really. Diesel's mother pretended to be a bruja to keep people out of her business, which was dealing drugs.

"Dalia came and took her baby. And Ma tried to scare her into giving it back."

"Why didn't she just call the cops? For once, the law would have probably been on her side," Manny teased.

Diesel chuckled. "I'm glad she took it. That kid cried all the time. Ma don't know how to take care of no baby. She was just in it for the check."

They both knew it was true. There was nothing else to say so they were silent for a while.

For want of something better to do, Diesel jumped up and slapped the top of the door casing. "Your shift is almost over; you want to get something to eat?" he asked.

Manny gave him a noncommittal shrug and walked over to lean against the open back door. It smelled rank—garbage and decaying food filled the dumpster—but the breeze was nice. He closed his eyes, took another drag, and then flicked the burning butt onto the damp alley floor. It kept burning. As he bowed his head to watch it, a thick curl of sandy hair fell forward like a shade over one eye. The flame was a thin red glow. He smashed it with the toe of his shoe. He didn't get Diesel. He knew what went on here, but he kept coming back and talking to him like he couldn't see how things were.

Diesel put his hand on Manny's shoulder. He flinched, surprised by the touch. "Manny?" Diesel asked.

"Maybe," he said. "I gotta cash out first."

"You want to smoke this first?" Diesel produced a fat, perfectly rolled doobie.

"Hell, yeah." Manny grinned.

Diesel lit it, made sure it was burning good before he passed it.

Manny took a long drag and held the smoke in. "Man, you should shave that shit off," he said, pointing to Diesel's sketchy mustache.

"What do you mean?" Diesel asked, smoothing the wispy hairs down as though it were a full-on Fu Manchu. "This is the shit. You know I look good."

Manny laughed, releasing a burst of smoke. He took another drag, shook his head, and laughed again, but he held the smoke in this time. Then he passed the joint back to Diesel. They continued this ritual in silence until the joint was a roach that Diesel could barely hold between his thick thumb and forefinger. He took one last hit, and then he flicked it away.

Manny pulled out a pack of cigarettes, shook one out, and offered it to Diesel. They both lit up.

"I could really go for a beer right now," Diesel said.

"Me too. We could go back in and get one." He looked at his watch. "I'm officially off."

"No, not here," Diesel said. Manny looked at him, waiting for more.

But Diesel just shook his head and said, "I just rather go someplace else."

"Why?" Manny wanted him to say it, to own up to knowing who and what he was.

"I just rather go somewhere else," Diesel repeated, but there was something else, something like a plea in his eyes.

Just then an older guy came to stand in the doorway. They both recognized him as a regular, one of the guys that came trolling for young boys.

"You almost done here, Manny?" he asked. "You got a few minutes?"

Diesel turned to the guy, and in a voice that had the impact of a fist, he said, "Get the fuck outta here."

"Oh, sorry. I see you're busy," the old guy said as he backed away with his hands up, to show that he didn't want any trouble.

"That's why," Diesel said. "That's fucking why."

"Fuck you!" Manny said and flicked his cigarette away.

"No," Diesel said as he put his hand to Manny's cheek. "Love me." And he leaned in carefully and pressed his lips gently to Manny's.

The Riverfront Bar and Grille

The Stevie Wonder sound-alike pressed the keys of his portable synthesizer as he mentally selected a cut from the greatest hits album. He shifted his feet on the tiny wooden stage, and his collapsible chair shuddered. Metallic tones tolled down the narrow aisle between the bar and the wine and dark-wood hues of the leather booths. "My *chérie amour*, pretty little girl that I adore. You're the only one my heart beats for." The pseudo Wonder leaned into the microphone, urging the notes forward, the insistent beat competing with the Riverfront's special—sizzling-hot Buffalo chicken wings—and the house white zinfandel.

Monday, an off night, Barbara and Persia sat at a table nearest the dance floor. Persia, who already had a buzz because she was two drinks up on Barbara, was looking around, gauging the male possibilities and humming to herself, while Barbara was just finishing her first drink.

"I don't care," Barbara was saying. "I don't care if he's got somebody else. He's still my husband."

"Look, for I don't know how long, you've been saying you were tired of his shit. How you felt he was holding you back. Now, you're half stepping when you can actually have your freedom and can get somebody you really want, somebody that might make you happy," Persia said.

"It's just that I'm used to him. And, well, he's a good father. It's hard being out here alone," Barbara said, trying to explain how confused she felt.

"You sound like your momma. When Scooter was cheating on me, your mother actually said, 'Men gon' be men. Sometimes

127

you just got to close your eyes and remember the good parts.' Pleeeze." Persia drew the last word out to show her disgust.

"That sounds like Momma," Barbara said, laughing and shaking her head. "And don't expect me to take up for Scooter because he was my brother. That's between y'all. But I gotta say, my husband does have some really good parts."

"Right. And according to you, he believes in sharing them. Copiously," Persia countered.

Barbara tipped her glass up to take a sip, but found that it was empty. After a minute, she said, "But he works hard, pays the bills."

"Just last week, you were laughing at him. Talking about he didn't know how to dress, walking around in corduroys, flannel shirts, and work boots all the time. You were sitting right there telling me and Yvonne how he didn't want nothing out of life, that he was just settling."

"But . . ," Barbara began.

"Sitting up there talking about how you were a material girl, a black woman who knew she was entitled to the American Dream, and how you were going to dump that tired man of yours as soon as the right benefactor came along," Persia teased her.

"Yeah." She laughed with Persia. "But he ain't come along yet, and it might get lonely waiting . . . Look, I'm going to the bathroom," Barbara said as she stood up and grabbed her purse.

A dark-brown-skinned girl leaned over, gently patting the frizzled ends of her hair. Barbara leaned farther into the mirror, applying the deep-purple lipstick, which was much too dark for her caramel complexion, but it was what everyone was wearing, and she liked its iridescent shine.

"It's so hot out there." The girl spoke in a thick West Indian accent.

"Especially on the dance floor," Barbara agreed, pressing her lips onto one of the coarse brown paper hand towels.

"I should get me a perm," the girl said as she mopped the sweat around her hairline with one of the paper towels.

Barbara looked at the girl's short hair and thought, *There wouldn't be much point*, but she gave the girl a smile anyway.

"Say, can I use some of your lipstick?" the girl asked.

"I'm sorry, I don't let people use my lipstick," Barbara answered as she dropped her lipstick into her purse, snapped the clutch closed, and headed back out to the bar.

Drew and his friend Oscar sat at their usual place at the end of the bar near the door, where they nursed a Courvoisier and a Long Island iced tea, respectively. There they could watch the ladies as they came in. They figured this gave them first crack at the most attractive young women. Even though neither could place in a Denzel contest, nice-looking girls often sought them out; the duo was just making it easy for them. Some of the women they knew very well having partied with them before. Others had heard rumors about a construction deal that Drew and Oscar were supposed to be working on that had something vaguely to do with Edsel or Henry Ford, or some City contract that they were sure to get because they were in good with Coleman. Either way, they were always greeted with exaggerated hugs, warm kisses, and overloud, friendly conversations. These perks made up for the icy gusts of wind that burst through the door every time a patron entered. On a good night, after the downtown offices closed, hordes of well-manicured lady attorneys, social workers, and office managers would come in, in clumps of twos and threes. Half turned toward the door, with only their backs in view, Drew and Oscar were always there to welcome them. Drinks in hand, they sat poised, waiting to be surprised by the next pair of darkly tinted lips parted to reveal a smile and a set of straight white teeth.

It didn't matter that Drew was more than a little overweight or that Oscar was no longer young or that both had been married and divorced a couple of times and that no one knew their current status—or that neither was particularly handsome. They both dressed well: tailored shirts, silk and linen blazers in the summer, superfine wool suits in winter, and the appropriate brightly colored power tie.

Most importantly, they had acquired a reputation for dealing with the big dogs. They had aligned themselves with the appropriate faction when Greektown was expanding and with the politically aligned cable company and sludge haulers when the City contracts were being awarded. It didn't really matter whether their end of the deal was ever realized because they could always secure a minor contract or temporary appointment to enable them to keep their running tab from being discussed with any anxiety.

Oscar was satisfied as long as he could hustle up enough to keep up the note on his condo at 1300, his leased Benz, and the American Express Gold Card that he kept in the front of his appointment book so that it was clearly visible when he opened it. Drew's main concerns were the cabin cruiser he kept docked at a marina off Jefferson and a ready vial of coke.

Although happy hour had come and gone, they still sat at the end of the bar. Most of the manicured up-and-coming ladies had headed home to their husbands, babies, or empty apartments to plan what they were going to wear to work the next day. Drew nursed his chilled cognac and Oscar his Long Island iced tea while scanning the club for leftovers. They were debating whether or not they should throw in the towel when Barbara came up behind Drew and tapped him on his shoulder.

He turned around to face her and broke into a smile.

Encouraged, she asked, "Aren't you Drew Mallett? I met you a few weeks ago at the mayor's birthday party."

His smile broadened; three or four hundred people had attended that overpriced Swedish meatball affair.

She stuck her hand out. "Barbara Miller."

He took her hand and held it, his thumb making circles in her palm.

She blushed and went on babbling, not knowing how to retrieve her hand.

"I was with my friend Persia. She works for the City ombudsman. Her boss gave her the tickets. You know all the City department heads have to buy them, and anyway he and his wife had already planned their vacation to Hawaii so he gave Persia the tickets." She knew she was babbling, but she couldn't seem to stop.

"That's Persia over there." She pointed to Persia, who stood pinned against a mirrored portion of the wall by a tall broadshouldered young man. His face was very near hers, and they looked like they were breathing words into each other's nostrils. Occasionally, Persia would tilt her head, and you could see a smile around the edges of her mouth.

"Remember?" Barbara was saying earnestly as she seized the opportunity to retrieve her hand when Drew turned to look at Persia.

"Sure, I remember. How could I forget a woman as beautiful as you?" he said, turning back to Barbara, who blushed appropriately.

"Have you met my friend, Oscar Grey?"

Oscar reached over, shook Barbara's hand, and issued a "Charmed" that sounded almost cynical.

"Why don't you sit here with us and have a drink?" Drew moved over and offered Barbara the stool between him and Oscar. "What are you drinking?"

"I'll have a Long Island iced tea," she said, sitting down.

"Jerry," Drew called to the bartender, "bring the lady an iced tea, and put it on my tab." He smiled at Barbara, who grinned back at him.

"What have you ladies got up for this evening?" Drew asked, offering Barbara a cigarette.

"No, thank you," she said. "We're not doing anything special. We just stopped in for a drink. Persia's celebrating a raise, and we just decided . . ." She ended with a shrug.

"That's great," intoned Oscar. "You should invite your friend over for a drink so we can help her celebrate."

"I don't know. She looks kind of busy," she said as she looked back over her shoulder at Persia.

Just then, the young man who had been occupying Persia's space so completely headed toward the men's room.

Drew waited a beat or two and then suggested, "You should ask her to come over. Tell her we've got something special in the car if she likes a little toot." Adding a gentle push just below her waist, he said, "Tell her if she can't come just now, she can meet us in the car. It's the silver Benz in the parking lot next door. She can't miss it. But tell her to hurry, or we'll be way ahead of her."

Barbara made her way around to Persia, who sat on a stool with her back against the bar, sipping her drink and smoking a cigarette.

"Girl, where you been?" Persia asked.

"Waiting for you to get tired of that big pretty thing breathing down your neck," Barbara said, grinning.

"Well, I hope you got a good pension plan." They laughed.

"Seriously though, before he gets back, I was over there with Drew Mallett . . ."

"Hmm. How'd you run into that?"

"I just went up to him and made him remember me from the mayor's birthday party, and he bought me a drink."

"I don't know how true it is, but he supposed to have some money. He supposed to have something to do with that new hotel they're building next to city hall."

"His friend Oscar something wants to meet you. He sent me over to get you to have a drink with us," said Barbara.

Persia looked back over her shoulder across the bar. Oscar was watching so she smiled. He nodded and tipped his glass to her.

"I didn't know he was so old," she said, frowning at Barbara. "I think you got the best one even if he is kind of fat."

"It's just a drink."

"I was just starting to get something going here . . . I don't know," Persia hedged.

"Look, you've been over here with that dude for nearly half an hour. Give him your number or take his. Y'all can get something going another time. Besides, you know our rule. We came together; we leave together. So you can't go home with him.

"Anyway, I wasn't going to tell you because you know I don't usually do it, but I think they got some coke and they want us to get high with them. Drew said if you can't come right now, you can meet us at the car," Barbara urged.

"OK, give me a minute." Persia sighed. "You go on ahead. I'll spend a little more time with my new cutie, give him my number, and then I'll meet you outside. Where's his car?"

"He said it's the silver Benz in the parking lot next door."

"I'm buzzing and feeling adventurous tonight. You tell them to save me some," said Persia.

Drew sat his heavy leather briefcase on his lap. From it he pulled a square sheet of clear plastic with blunted edges. He spread the white powder onto the sheet, and using his driver's license as a scraper, he shaped the coke into several inch-long lines. Then he rolled a ten-dollar bill into a tight cylinder and handed it and the plastic sheet to Barbara. Before they had completed one round, Persia was banging on the window and whispering loudly, "Wait for me." Oscar laughed, squeezed his nose, inhaled, then passed the sheet back to Barbara and unlocked the door. Persia slid into the front seat next to Oscar. Then she reached into the back seat and gingerly tugged at the sheet Barbara was holding and said, "Girl, you don't know what you're doing. Pass that up here." Barbara laughed, snorted another line, and then handed the sheet up to Persia.

"Y'all want to go down to the boat?" Drew asked between snorts. Barbara sat back in the seat, enjoying the firmness of the leather upholstery and feeling quite regal as the clean, crisp edge of the coke spread over her and assured her she was having a good time and that all was right with the world.

"Let's go," Persia sang out, and Oscar started the motor.

The four of them sat on the deck of the boat buzzing, sipping cognac, and listening to the radio as the Electrifying Mojo segued into the Quiet Storm. The pristine midnight blue of the sky, the river, and the Storm's continuous flow of R&B love songs soothed while the cognac warmed. The conversation was light as soft laughter bracketed quiet debates about who sang what Motown love song and when. This was a topic about which Drew knew a great deal so Oscar sat back and let him dazzle the ladies with his knowledge. The ladies were dutifully impressed and sang his praises. Barbara leaned against Drew with her stocking feet tucked under her dress as he tactically rested one hand on her behind while the other ran tentatively over one of her breasts. Persia and Oscar sat in the deck chairs facing each other at a distance.

Before long, Drew led Barbara below deck to a large padded bench where he tried to undress her between what he would have called deep, soulful kisses. Barbara wondered whether she should play hard to get. She wasn't even sure she liked this man, who'd worked his way into her bra and whose chubby fingers were toying roughly with her nipples.

But she hadn't been with a man in weeks, not since before her husband moved out. So, she let him touch her. She liked the man smell and weight of him. And while he was a little clumsy, she could tell that he was trying to be gentle.

The sound of water lapping against the boat and the gentle rock, rock, rocking was pleasing. Briefly, she wondered what he thought of her. She worried that he might think she did this kind of thing all of the time. Abruptly, she sat up and shook her head as she held the front of her dress up in an effort to conceal her bare breasts, "No."

He stopped, letting her breathe. He was used to this hesitancy, used to them having second thoughts right before he sealed the deal. But he could tell from the way this one breathed and squirmed beneath him that she was attainable. He let his lips brush hers, gently, tilted his forehead to hers, and then began again with much more persistence and greater intensity. Before long, he had her pantyhose wadded up in a corner, her gauzy summer dress wound around her waist, and the flesh of his massive thighs was plop, plop, plopping against her slim, naked ones as he sank deeper and deeper.

It was wrong, she didn't know this man, but it felt good to have a man inside her. And the coke, cognac, and rhythm of the rocking boat made it all seem surreal. But even as she lifted her legs to curl them up around his hips so that she could receive him more completely, she knew this man could never mean anything to her and that he had brought her here for this purpose. The slap and slide of skin against skin caused a tremor to spread up through the center of her body; her fingers dug into his arms. She closed her eyes and thrust up to meet him, shivering as he slid deeper. Maybe this was why she had come; maybe this was what she needed.

Meanwhile Persia sat on the deck of the boat, a safe distance from the leering Oscar. Both were listening to the plop, plop, plopping of the couple fucking in the cabin below.

Finally, Persia said, "I'm hungry. What have you guys got to eat?"

"Sweet meat," Oscar answered, grinning at her.

"I meant something appetizing," Persia threw back at him without missing a beat as she turned up the radio and Stevie's "Boogie On Reggae Woman" moved into its fast-paced instrumental chorus.

"The Riverfront Bar and Grille" first appeared in *Of Burgers & Barrooms: Stories & Poems*. Charlotte, NC: Main Street Rag, 2017.

Persia Dunne

*The new-world Christ will need consummate skill to
walk up the waters where huge bubbles burst.*

Sometimes I park at the bottom of a hill that's all hay-colored
clumps of grass, crags littered with brittle bits of newspaper, pop
bottles, and Styrofoam burger wrappers. There are stairs that
begin at the base of the hill and go up, up, up forever until they
finally lose themselves in traffic and tall buildings. Unseasoned
climbers stop periodically to breathe, and by midway their
breathing is ragged and hoarse. In winter, it puffs out in shallow
clouds the color of fog.

Midway, the cold rasps my throat. As I stop to fill my lungs,
I lean over the rail and look down at the washed-out red shingles
of the Interfaith Shelter that hovers over the blackened hull of
a clapboard row house. Nearby, the sculpted cornice of an oversized brick building that now houses the Street Academy gives
the foot of this hill a sense of legacy like the blues giving birth
to the Motown sound, a progression of use that offers a fragile
comfort, a glimpse of hope.

Bright white towers of plastic and tinted glass loom at
the top of the hill, and a mammoth Grecian temple swells the
left angle of my peripheral vision. Its clean stone pillars instill
fright. I linger longer than necessary on the snow-dampened
expanse of wooden planks, wondering if it's worth it to
go on.

Do you hear the rustle of chameleons in the cane?

When Persia was born and they put that bundle of pink flannel, with its tiny pale fists and yawning face, in my arms, I knew she was in for trouble. I just wasn't sure whether she'd be the cause of it or it would come to her.

She was always New York; ain't never really been Detroit. Even though she light skinned, she got this long egg-shaped face like those Africans they used to have in the *National Geographic* when they did stories on places like the Sahara and the Sudan. Those people with yellowish clay painted on they faces and lilac-stained lost-looking eyes. It make her look exotic like those ladies in those painting by that Modigliani guy, but not white, only almost.

And she was always doing something different with her hair. When everybody was wearing pageboys, she cut hers all off, put a straightener in it, and wore it in this boyish style with tiny curls that trailed down her neck like shiny black rings of tinsel. I didn't like her cutting all of her hair off like that, but it was sort of becoming. It was a lot better than them long, fuzzy, snake-looking things she started growing on her head that one time. I couldn't stand them things; she called them dreadlocks. She was the first person I'd ever seen with that hairstyle. I've seen a few people with them since, but Persia had done something different with hers. They had thin, fuzzy strands of gold and platinum mixed in with her natural brown. She used to tell people who didn't know no better that she was born with the color like that, that it was like a birthmark. Anyway, by the time I got used to the fuzzy tubes, she had changed it to something else.

In the summer, she used to wear these thin leather sandals, all beat-up looking like she found them in a secondhand store, and these loose-fitting cotton dresses with crazy prints that would cling to her bare breasts and behind. When it started getting cold, she'd put on these wool tights and heavy sweaters with skirts that hung past her calves. I used to always have to get on her about hiking them skirts up around her hips when she went to get on her ten-speed. She used that bike to get around most of the time, until the bitter cold set in, and then she would get one of her many admirers, men and women, to take her places. I used to wonder how she attracted all them rich kids driving they daddies' Mercedes when she dressed like somebody's rag doll.

Persia ain't never been one to act like something she wasn't, and she knew she was poor. If all we had was beans in the house for weeks, she was the first to get to washing the beans. Then she'd go find some onions to dice up for spice. She ain't never put on no funny airs like some folks' kids do. I be seeing them at the mall poking they lip out cause they momma cain't afford to buy them the brand they want. And when Persia would come sit on the porch with me or Belle, she would listen like what we had to say was interesting to her. But I have heard her on the phone with her friends rounding out her words, talking that proper talk and sounding like one of them Kennedys. And I have seen how she treat them sons of judges, and doctors and whatnot, how she act like she was the mistress of the orchard and they was just one of the many apples anxious to drop in her lap or fall near her feet hoping to be picked, to be nibbled next.

She would make them wait for what seemed like hours while she'd be taking pictures of some dying weed out in the backyard. Sometimes she would just change her mind about going out with them after they had been waiting at the door all dressed and anxious. I figured she knew who she could and couldn't do that to. She didn't act like that when she was with Scooter. Sure, she would wear them country-looking dresses or come in with her hair all over her head in some wild style, but Scooter—George was his given name, and that's what she called him—he had that girl tamed. And when they was together, she wasn't hanging around all them artsy-fartsy whiteys and uppity niggahs, talking all proper. She just started that stuff since he been gone.

There is a sharp click as she fits into her chair and draws it to the table.

Lexington Avenue, Manhattan. Early evening, just past twilight. I didn't know that they had Indian summer in New York. Ahead someone is laughing and speaking in Chinese, and a passing couple is arguing in French. Hawkers in pink-bibbed aprons hustle men into uptown nudie nightclubs while a saxophone whines across the street, the velvet of its carrying case spread wide and littered with dollar bills. Long limousines slide up to the Waldorf Astoria, expelling fur coats and tailored trenches. A stroll away, the MoMA and Brother's Stereo & Tape Decks, each respecting the other's role in the world of art.

Like the chameleon, one must learn to be all things to all people, to give them what they want even when they can't say what that is. It has to become a reflex action, and it can be very tiring.

"Marry me, Persia." He hands it to me, a little velvet box, pride and pleasure all over his face.

"I love you, Persia." And he kisses me full on the lips like he's taking a drink. He even swallows afterward. I smile up at him, trying to sustain his pleasure, and then I open the box. There's a ruby dead center, suffocated in diamond petals. This ring has transcended gaudy and is violently bleeding into garish. A part of me is pleased that he didn't go for the traditional marquise or emerald cut; he sees me as different. I should be flattered, but he really overshot. Makes me wonder how people see me, or at least what they think they see. But the stones are genuine, and if the need arises, it promises a good resale value. I touch the hard stone in the center with the tip of my index finger. No barmaid's apron for me, no sleeping in cardboard boxes, not as long as I have some soul left to sell.

Immediately, I reprimand myself and try to sense the look on my face, wondering if he can see my thoughts.

I smile up at him. "It's too much, thank you."

He is really a nice man, good to me. Tolerant. But he has no lips, just a slit, a gash, where his mouth should be. I offer him mine, and again, he swallows.

Arms of the audience reach out, grab and hold her.
Claps are steel fingers that manacle her wrists and move
them forward to acceptance.

For all her strangeness, she always acted regular until she went up
there and married that chicken-smelling white man. When he
come around, it put me in mind of when I be cutting up a chick-
en. Remind me of how that cold, slippery, gooey skin feel. How it
feel all slimy when I ease my thumb up under it, near the grizzle,
to loosen it up before I try to cut through. I cain't stand it when
my knife hit the bone. Anyway, white people smell like that: raw,
like chicken. It make me sick to my stomach when I have to be
around too many at once, like on a elevator or something. I don't
see how she can stand it, being with him all the time like that,
sleeping with him, smelling raw chicken all the time.

Last time she came home to visit, we was sitting there
watching *Family Feud*. The category was status symbols, and we
started screaming out the clues like we always used to. So, I
hollered Cadillac, fur coat. She shouted window, parking space,
and I look at her real funny and say, "What you talking about?
Every house got a window." She start laughing, laughing at me
like I done missed out on the biggest joke in the world. Later on,
she explain how in some companies only the big shot got windows, and the secretaries and like that get stuck in dark cubby
holes. She say that man she married to got a whole wall full of
windows that go from the floor to the ceiling. But she hurt my
feelings the way she laughed at me like she knew something I
couldn't never know. She never done that before.

I am weak with much giving.

We have a very nice apartment. There are handwoven rugs on
our doorsteps, and pieces from our travels are placed carelessly
on the mantle. In the living room, near the divan there is a
Miró, an angular, roughly hewn black object. We are high above

the city, and sometimes at night, I step out onto the terrace and take deep breaths of whirling siren screams, people shouts, and crisp neon.

Gershwin is not authentic enough for him. He says that if I want to listen to black music, I should listen to the real thing, and he plays Screamin' Jay Hawkins, Jelly Roll Morton, Monk or Parker and Billie. He has studied them. But I like Gershwin's celebration of life and Puccini's pain too. He likes to lay his head in my lap while he listens and tells me what some critic or professor has chosen to label the intricate chords and rhythms. My finger trails along his wispy hairline, it lingers momentarily at his temples, and my face smiles down at him as he defines me.

This is a safe place. There's a doorman, and here, hunger is unthinkable. To pass the time, I browse the shops picking up flavored coffees, exotic fruits, and tins of candies with foreign labels that I store in the backs of kitchen cabinets.

He is attentive, reaches for my hand when we cross city streets and even when we're not. Tells me how beautiful my skin is, how beautiful our children will be. I listen and laugh and encourage him to come, to come inside me, but I don't want his children. I am not going to have his mutant children. Half-white and confused, prep school voices coming out of full lips . . . not out of my body. No matter how he begs and strokes and feathers my bush with licks and kisses.

I remember once before I married this man, when I was living with George, I had on this blond wig and I was primping in the bathroom mirror. I thought it looked rather nice, sexy. So I called George in to show him. He looked at me with this frown on his face. Then he pulled it off my head, said something like, "You think that shit's cute? Baby, you got too much going for you to be messing it up with they shit." At the time, I laughed and put it back on, but I never wore it out of the house because it didn't look right after that. Didn't fit. So I'll be this white man's wife. I'll even wear his garish ring, but I won't dilute my blood.

*Her words have no feel to them. They are pink petals
that fall upon the velvet cloth.*

She talking bout getting her tubes tied. Ain't even thirty, never
even had no kids, and newly married. She say that's why. Don't
want no kids with this man. I tell her maybe you won't be with
him forever. Maybe sometime you'll have another husband, and
he'll want kids, and you'll want his. She say she don't want no
mistakes. Don't want no diluted baby mutants. I ask her what's a
mutant, and she say something that ain't supposed to be. I know
she shouldn't a married that chicken-smelling man.

*God is a small black boy, timidly pulling at the preach-
er's coattail.*

Sometimes I wonder is it enough. If not, what is? Something
is missing, and I really miss George, who is, of course, dead.
But what is dead? Can people die if you still think about them
and need them? Are they dead just because others say they
are? He kept me on line, kept me grounded. When he was
alive, he was always on my case about what was real, what was
important, helping me to figure out how to measure it. When
I got confused, we used to talk it out. I'd complain about us
not having a decent car or that we needed a new bedroom
suite, or at least a bed, because the mattress and box spring
we were sleeping on sat on the bare floor. He'd say, "Baby, we
don't need none of that. That's what they want, us to become
slaves to things, slaves to their culture. We don't need any of
it. As long as we got enough to eat, a place to sleep, and each
other—we are ahead of the game." I would laugh and say,
"But it sure would be nice to have a washing machine so we
wouldn't have to lug these clothes down three flights of stairs
and up the street to the Laundromat." He'd just laugh and say,
"It's good for us."

The click is metallic like the sound of a bolt being shot into place.

She was by here yesterday. Said she missed me, she missed home. So she came in on the red-eye with her husband. He had some work to do here in town. They was staying downtown at one of them big hotels. She looked real nice in that dress, but the color was a little too light for her. Seem like she just faded into it; lost some weight too. Didn't eat much either; she usually clean me out when she come home. Something was wrong, but she not talking.

Each one is a bolt that shoots into a slot, and is locked there.

This balcony both terrifies and fascinates me. I was never very good at double Dutch. When I tried to jump in, I used to always get hit by the . . . thud . . . thud . . . of the rope. After a while, just the blur of the ropes twirling scared me. They seemed to move so fast and fall so hard. But I like the songs and the rhythm, and I used to play with the girls who jumped rope sometimes when they had only one rope or, better yet, if it was just a hand-clapping game.

> Little Sally Walker
> Sitting in a saucer

So the girls wouldn't know I was afraid, I used to cultivate this I'm-too-busy look. When they played double Dutch, I'd pretend to read or bring out my blackboard and play teacher on the porch.

> Rise Sally rise
> Wipe your weeping eyes

Most times, the girls on the block didn't pay any attention to me, but as we got older and they outgrew jump ropes and patty-cake, they began to come up onto the porch to see what I was doing. By then, I had expanded my pursuits.

> Put your hand on your hips
> and let your backbone flip

After they broke the ice by asking what book I'd been reading, we started fixing each other's hair, polishing each other's fingernails, or debating the best way to hike up a skirt without getting too much bulge around the waist. But mostly, we discussed boys.

> All shake it the east
> All shake it to the west

And then it was like everyone paired off or got pregnant. Black women, unlike black men, rarely look outside of their race for a mate. Maybe they like staying close to home, or maybe when it comes to men they disagree with the American ideal of beauty and desirability. During the Movement, it was about tribe building, bringing black babies into the world to bolster our numbers. Some Sisters swore they'd never sleep with a white man because during slavery and beyond too many of us had been taken against our will by white men. But back when we were all pairing up, it wasn't about prescribed values or cultural preservation. It was about what felt good. It was chemical. And anyway, I got George.

> All shake it to the very one
> that you love the best.

The street is way, way down there, a thin strip of concrete alongside a wide strip of black tar littered with white lines and yellow cabs. This brick railing, thick and hard, is something I can hold on to.

I met my husband in that bodega down there on that far corner. It's not really a bodega, but it specializes in imported foods. I was pricing the canned asparagus when he came up to me. He did an obvious double take, and then he actually walked around me in sort of a circle. I thought his approach was kind of cute, but he didn't really appeal to me so I turned my back to him and continued reading the can.

"You're a real beauty," he whispered into my ear from behind me.

I didn't look up. I thought he was weirdly aggressive so I took a few steps away from him.

"How about some coffee?" He stepped closer, consuming the space I'd put between us.

"In a public place," he added when I didn't respond. "I don't do this kind of thing often." He stood his ground, gave me a boyish grin, and showed me his palms in that *see, I'm harmless* gesture. I couldn't help but smile.

Maybe he saw the smile, or maybe it was just his natural persistence, but a half hour later we stood on this very terrace sipping Sea Breezes with Michael Frank's *Art of Tea* bouncing in the background.

It was a long time before I let him touch me. I kind of liked talking to him—he would go on and on trying to impress me with what he knew, where he'd been, what he'd done, who he'd met. I would just smile and nod. He seemed to like it that way . . . the role of teacher . . . no, mentor, to my wide-eyed protégé. That part was easy. The touching was hard.

I didn't like his scent. Not that he smelled bad exactly, not like Momma says—raw chicken, but different, foreign. For a while, I'd buy him colognes—Aramis, Lagerfeld, the ones that George used to wear. But they didn't blend well with his natural scent so I gave up and just tried to get used to him. Besides, I wasn't seeing anyone else, and he was good to me—generous and attentive.

So I started by letting him kiss my breasts—practice at getting a rise out of my nipples. Then later, I let him kiss my neck and, much later, my lips. When I let him touch my clitoris, he got overexcited and scratched me. The hurt look on his face touched me so that when he asked if he could kiss it and make it better, I let him.

When I let him in the first time, he came so quickly that if not for his embarrassment I wouldn't have known he'd come.

Once he actually made me come. He was on me breathing hard and pushing himself into me in his usual rhythm. I turned my head away and closed my eyes like I always do because it helps me to concentrate on the stroke, the feeling inside me, rather than who I'm with. All of a sudden, he gripped my ass real tight and began thrusting himself into me hard and steady. And he kept saying, "It's all mine. Tell me it's all mine." Just like George used to. All at once, I came and cried and cried and came. But that was the only time. I remember him asking me afterward, as he hovered over me and I lay dazed beneath him, "Persia, you do love me, don't you?" And I answered, with my eyes still closed, "Yeah baby, I love you." He rolled onto his back and I lay my head on his chest, listening to his heart as he secured me to him.

> *Soon the audience will paint your dusk faces white, and call you beautiful.*

Epigraphs in this story are excerpts from *Cane* by Jean Toomer (1923), with the exception of "God is a small black boy . . ." from "Roselily" in *In Love and Trouble* by Alice Walker (1967).

About the Author

Esperanza Cintrón is the author of three books of poetry: *Chocolate City Latina*, the Naomi Long Madgett Award–winner *What Keeps Me Sane*, and *Visions of a Post-Apocalyptic Sunrise*. A native Detroiter and Afro Latina of Puerto Rican descent, she is co-founder of the Sisters of Color Writers Collective and the creator of its literary journal *Seeds*, for which she served as editor until 2006. Cintrón holds a doctorate in English literature and has been awarded a Michigan Council for the Arts Individual Artist Grant, *The Metro Times* Poetry Prize, and Callaloo Creative Writing Fellowships at Oxford and at Brown Universities. Under the nom de plume Alegra Verde she has written a number of short stories and novellas that have been published as ebooks and in anthologies. She teaches literature, writing, and film at a college in downtown Detroit. *Shades: Detroit Love Stories* is her first collection of fiction.